SI
SILENCE

By the same author

Ahi is an aspiring publisher and wishes to make it big someday. When her favourite author's autobiography lands on her table – which has confessions of his heinous crimes, illegal businesses and few eminent others as his partners in crime – she doesn't know if it's real or someone's trap.

It could get her a big breakthrough, but little does she know that it would turn her world upside down completely.

Her morbid curiosity pulls her into the depth of a conspiracy. She finds herself at the centre of various mishaps and murders, as if someone wants to lead the way. Driven by her childhood friend Samim's encouragement, and watched over by the ever so charming ACP Rathore, she has to jeopardize her life to find the brutal truth of her past.

Touching, thrilling and deeply mysterious, *Sin is the New Love* is the journey of a girl who stumbles upon the truth about her origin while chasing her dream.

THE SINFUL SILENCE

ABIR MUKHERJEE

Srishti
PUBLISHERS & DISTRIBUTORS

Srishti Publishers & Distributors
A unit of AJR Publishing LLP
212A, Peacock Lane
Shahpur Jat, New Delhi – 110 049
editorial@srishtipublishers.com

First published by
Srishti Publishers & Distributors in 2021

Copyright © Abir Mukherjee, 2021

10 9 8 7 6 5 4 3 2 1

This is a work of fiction. The characters, places, organizations and events described in this book are either a work of the author's imagination or have been used fictitiously. Any resemblance to people, living or dead, places, events, communities or organizations is purely coincidental.

The author asserts the moral right to be identified as the author of this work.

All rights reserved. No part of this publication may be reproduced, stored in a retrieval system, or transmitted, in any form or by any means, electronic, mechanical, photocopying, recording or otherwise, without the prior written permission of the Publishers.

Printed and bound in India

*Dedicated to every person
with a red line under their names
in MS Word.*

Acknowledgments

I would like to thank my family for their continuous support in all phases of my life.

Thanks to Mr Jayanta Kumar Bose, Mr Arup Bose and Srishti Publishers & Distributors for having faith in me and giving me the opportunity to be published with their esteemed publication house.

Thanks to my editor, Stuti Gupta. Without you, a bundle of pages wouldn't have become a book.

Thanks to my lady brigade – Panchali Ganguly, Sucharita Bhowmik, Sanhita Majumder, Debashree Bhattacharyya and Sayantani Banerjee for their help and encouragement in different phases of writing.

A sincere thanks to all my readers. I am humbled and honoured. Truly, I love you all. I appreciate every read, every clap and every response. I take absolutely nothing for granted. These are gifts you give to me of your own free and generous will. I cherish them. Thank you.

It was 10 p.m. The wind howled and at times groaned in agony like a despairing lover, while rushing through the streets and alleys of Noida. Anything not nailed down was blown along in its melancholy. Dry leaves, dust, papers and plastic swirled in the air like confetti. The rain unshackled herself from the charcoal cloud and pounded on the ground, embracing the wind. A jagged bolt of lightning ripped the dark sky into pieces as that behemoth cloud roared in anger.

The brilliant flash of lightning pierced the darkness inside Abhimanyu's drawing room. He squinted, frowning on his couch as his eyes had adjusted to that gloominess. He chuckled and cast his eyes back on a capsule on the centre table in front of him. He held the pill in a pinch, placed it on his tongue and swallowed it.

The more brutal the storm became outside, the calmer his brain got. He closed his eyes, lounging himself on the couch, and waited for that nirvana state. The magical dust inside the capsule's shell and lysergic acid diethylamide had reached his stomach.

A few weeks back, Abhimanyu had busted a racket of drug peddlers and managed to grab some of those hallucinogenic drugs. He had enjoyed his LSD trip, which was incomparably more pleasurable than his experience of alcohol, cocaine or marijuana.

He opened his eyes as he felt a chill rush through his spine, kicking open his brain to an infinite hollowness. He sensed the existence of his body like a buoyant feather in the air. His empty mind led him to gaze at the bright lights and vibrant hues in every nook and cranny of that room with childish amusement. The furniture, wall-clock, photo frames, refrigerator and all other objects in the room started melting in their orbs slowly. The walls began to float in a lethargic rhythm. He waved at Ahi, standing at the door of their bedroom in her favourite floral yellow frock. Some unknown red and white flowers were printed on it. Ahi had told him the names of those flowers a while ago, but he couldn't remember them anymore. He chuckled and smiled. She looked like a nymph, evolved from an illuminated wide opening of another world behind her.

"Happy birthday, love! See, I have been waiting for you for so long," he mumbled dizzily, gluing his eyes to Ahi's, sparkling in tears.

He stood up from the couch on his quivering legs. He felt the heat of that orb around Ahi as she came near him. She caressed his face, brought her face closer to his right ear and whispered, "Where is my gift?"

There was a benign and mumsy comfort in that familiar fragrance of Ahi.

"Haven't you seen it yet? It's on the dining table; your birthday cake," he said softly and tardily, trying hard to refrain his tongue from twisting. "White-forest with pineapple toppings and chocolate base. Your favourite, isn't it?" he asked, sandwiching her palm in between his. He felt an abnormal frostiness on her skin.

She nodded. Her rosy, heart-shaped lips were stretched, but not enough to form a spontaneous smile. It hinted a smirk. Her expressive, bluish-green eyes were expressing her pleasantness, but some pain overcast them with tears. The reddish tip of her nose and earlobes were trying hard to hush up some humiliation and brutality.

"Hey, aren't you happy?" His voice drowned in a crackly thunder. She kept quiet, wiping off the disguise of happiness from her face. Tears rolled down on her cheeks and perched between her lips. He wiped the tears, but it made a stain of blood on her face.

"What happened? Why are you bleeding?" He almost screamed, trembling. He noticed other wounds and bruises all over her.

"Don't you know it, Abhi?" she asked numbly and kissed on his forehead.

Suddenly, Abhimanyu felt a mighty blow in the core of his brain, and everything around him turned into boundless darkness. He collapsed on the floor.

"*Chal bhaunk!*" Chaddha responded after receiving the call from one of his informers.

"Arrey Chaddha ji, I have delegated all my boys for your information only, and you are talking to me like that! *Dhande ki maa behen ho gayi aaj*, do you know that?" Chakra, the informer, complained.

"Chakra, aren't you talking too much? Don't forget! Your drug peddling file is still with me," Chaddha snapped back.

"Sir, let me remind you that your boss Abhimanyu is my regular customer," Chakra replied calmly.

"*Teri maa ki...*" Chaddha burst in anger. "Okay, tell me now," he asked decently, not jeopardizing the thinnest chance to rescue two innocent girls.

Chaddha grabbed a piece of paper and jotted down the address Chakra narrated. He called Abhimanyu immediately after disconnecting.

Abhimanyu's mobile rang on the centre table, partially defeating his drawing room's gloominess before becoming silent. He groaned in disgust.

"Ahi, please pick up the phone," he blabbered, as it rang for the second time. He frowned, groped for his mobile on the centre table and pushed the phone accidentally from it to fall on the floor. He dragged himself on the floor and pushed up his body with the support of his strong hands. The bright light of the screen dazed him as he picked up the phone.

"Who is this?" he asked drowsily, somehow managing to receive the call.

"Good evening, Abhimanyu! Purshottam Sastri speaking," a calm and heavy voice responded. The syndicate was the brainchild of Purshottam Sastri, the most trusted and intimate friend of the coeval MP of Noida constituency. Despite not having any political position in the ruling party or any influential government post, he had an immense influence on the MP's decisions. By profession, he was a businessman, the owner of the Brindavan group of hotels and malls and head of the group of all business tycoons and industrialists of Noida. Without his blessings, no business deal could see the light of the real market, and that was his weapon, giving him the control to draw the political map of Noida. Behind the curtain, he was the kingmaker, the master of influencing people to do his dirty business while keeping his cuffs the cleanest. He was a venomous monster beneath the skin of a calm, composed and divine monk.

"Yes, sir."

"Sometimes, we need to kill our own dogs when they try to be our master. These four daring rebels were quite handy for the syndicate. However, greed incited them on the wrong path, against the syndicate. I have set the stage for you; you just need to do your duty like an honest police officer," Purshottam explained. His voice had an inhuman tranquillity.

"Okay, sir."

"Chakra would have exposed their location to your department by now. Best of luck, my golden boy!"

Abhimanyu had a look at his mobile screen as he heard a beeping sound and said, "Yes, they are trying to reach me." Purshottam disconnected the call.

"Sir, we know their location and we are starting right away. It's already 2 a.m., and we can't afford to delay by a single moment. We will pick you up on the way," Chaddha updated him in a single breath.

"Hmm... Okay!"

Chaddha banged the accelerator as soon as their SUV touched the main street, rain pattering noisily on the windshield. Chaddha had to depend on his conjectures and experiences because the wipers were failing to cut the thick curtain of water on the windscreen. Abhimanyu always relied on Chaddha to handle the steering wheel. He knew the short routes and lanes of Noida so well, and his calm head and impeccable control behind the wheels was remarkable.

Abhimanyu took the front seat beside the driver, followed by a few policemen and a policewoman on the back seats.

"How reliable is this information?" Abhimanyu asked, rolling the window down and pushing his face out. Raindrops kissed his face along with the chilled wind. He felt much better and refreshed.

"It's concrete. Chakra's information never fails," Chaddha said, glancing at Abhimanyu before moving his eyes back on the street. "They captured those girls somewhere in the slum in sector five. One of Chakra's men will guide us to the exact spot," he added.

"Hmm... What's the size of the gang?" Abhimanyu enquired, examining his favourite Glock 17, 9 mm, semi-automatic pistol. Due to his faint vision under the influence of drugs, he rubbed it over his palm.

Chaddha was well aware of Abhimanyu's addiction, so he ignored Abhimanyu's weird fumble and updated him, "Five... approximately. But we have a bigger problem." He took a pause to make a U-turn carefully and added, "We are not sure whether they are armed or not."

"That's not a problem, Chaddha ji; that's an opportunity to clean the society," Abhimanyu said gently. He pulled the magazine out from the gun and counted bullets, rubbings his thumb on it.

Chaddha knew what that meant, but wasn't sure how the half-baked information they had could help clean the society. "Sir, it can be dangerous. We should have clear information about their strength," he commented.

Abhimanyu pushed the magazine back with a clack and replied, "When life doesn't give us a choice, we are compelled to make the difficult decision because that's the only option. We are not sure, that's why we have the gun... to shoot them for our safety."

A heavy silence hung inside the vehicle. They all knew what was waiting for them, except the newly-appointed officer on the back seat. He asked, "Do you mean a planned encounter, sir?"

Questioning Abhimanyu's decision wouldn't have been a pleasant experience for that novice. Fortunately, Abhimanyu couldn't hear the question, and Chaddha took that opportunity to divert the topic. He exclaimed, "God knows, whether those girls are still safe."

"The ages of those two girls are twenty and twenty-seven and no demand of ransom has been made even after fifteen hours of kidnapping, which clearly point to the intention of the kidnapping – rape or sex trafficking," the new appointee at the back seat said.

Abhimanyu heard him clearly this time and turned back. But his vision was blurred enough to recognize nothing but two illuminated eyeholes of that officer in the dark.

"If the intention is only rape, we can expect only their corpses now." After a pause, he said, "They might still be alive in case of sex trafficking as the trading of a sex-slaves demands time; sometimes more than a day," he added.

"Who are you?" Abhimanyu asked, frowning.

"Vayu Iyer, IPS officer from Madurai, joined the unit yesterday as your backup, sir," he introduced himself steadily then fumbled, "Or sir... ji?"

"Backup? Hmm...." Abhimanyu exchanged a glance with Chaddha, smirking.

The rain had become significantly lighter when they reached sector five. They parked their vehicle at a distance and approached the location. A wet breeze welcomed them, as one of Chakra's men guided them through the narrow, dark and dingy alleys of that slum and showed them a house slightly larger than the other houses around it.

"Sir, my job is done. Please put in a word to Chakra bhai. He always assigns this kind of *chutya* work to me. *Kuchh* daring *kaam karna hai*," the man pleaded to Chaddha, almost whispering.

Chaddha glared at him for a second before slapping him violently. "Bhenchod, being a police officer, I will recommend you for a bigger crime? Bhag madarchod!" Chaddha whispered.

The man left, rubbing the cheek where four of Chaddha's fingerprints were vivid.

Abhimanyu gestured at two of his men and the woman to reach the back side of that house and stay alert. He pulled out his gun, tucked it inside the back of his jeans, and approached the house's entrance, tiptoeing. Vayu, Chaddha and Dubey followed him stealthily, holding their guns firmly.

An old man was lying on his small bed of jute-sacks in the corridor. He hummed along with an evergreen, old Bollywood song, '*Yeh raaten yeh mausam, nadi ka kinara*' on his radio. But, the sound of their gun cocking startled him. He hustled on his jute-sacks to stand up and stumbled on his radio. The song stopped.

Abhimanyu rushed to him, leaned his face close, and whispered, "I like this song. Play it!"

The old man fumbled in the dark to tune his radio back to the same station. Abhimanyu wondered if that interruption in the song could have made the abductors alert.

"Don't change the channel or volume," he admonished the old man, placing the gun barrel on his head.

The radio started playing again. *'Yeh baahon mein baahen, yeh behki nigahen...'*

Abhimanyu and his team took position at both sides of the door. Abhimanyu kicked open the door on the count of three and rushed into the room. The bright light inside the room dazed his eyes for a few seconds. To his surprise, he felt a violent strike on the left of his head, and everything blacked out in front of him. He groped on the nearest wall behind him, hearing scuffles, groaning, Chaddha's indecent shouting and sounds of objects breaking around him. After a jiffy headshake, his eyes caught up with a monochromatic vision of the room.

"Chaddha!" He shouted in anger, glancing at all the entwined human silhouettes in the room.

"Sir ji!"

Abhimanyu fired at lightning speed, aiming at the silhouette that hadn't responded to him. The song on the radio went on. Abhimanyu swung his gun and aimed at the three other silhouettes. Vayu held two of the abductors' necks in armlocks. Vayu ducked in a hurry, comprehending Abhimanyu's intention. Abhimanyu's gun roared again twice. The last kidnaper shook himself free from Dubey's grasp and rushed towards the door, which instead helped Abhimanyu to identify him distinctly. Abhimanyu shot him in his back without even looking at him.

Abhimanyu somehow managed to come out of that room, stumbling over the floor. He took a deep breath on reaching the narrow alley and lit a cigarette.

Chaddha and Dubey, along with the other two policemen, found a secret chamber in that house. Those two naked, raped and brutally tortured victims huddled as the lady constable entered that chamber with a pair of blankets.

"We could have arrested them."

Abhimanyu recognized the voice. He reluctantly glanced at Vayu, a lean and tall but toughly-built IPS officer. He had a sharp nose, a defined jaw line, high cheekbones beneath his dusky skin and a pair of lotus-shaped eyes. His crew cut hair made his thick moustache and kempt beard more prominent.

"We could have given them a chance to correct their mistakes. They might have evolved as better people after serving their imprisonment," Vayu commented further on Abhimanyu's chilling silence. "Moreover, we are not supposed to kill anyone except for self-defence. Our job is to arrest the suspects, take them to court and furnish the case with evidences and witnesses to earn the justice; not to deliver justice on the spot," Vayu continued, calmly staring at Abhimanyu's blank eyes.

"According to Criminal Procedure Code Section 46(1) and (2), if the suspect forcibly resists the endeavour to arrest or attempts to evade the arrest, such police officer may take all necessary action to result in the arrest. However, nothing in this section gives a right to kill...." Vayu was cut short by Abhimanyu.

"Look at them!" Abhimanyu ordered, pointing at those girls wrapped in blankets as the lady officer brought them out into the alley. Vayu looked back at Abhimanyu after catching a glimpse of those victims.

"Don't you think they deserve to live a normal life much more than those bastards?" Vayu attempted to speak something, but Abhimanyu raised his hand to stop him. "Arresting them doesn't make any sense to me. They will threaten those girls and their families not to speak up in court, and they will get away with it after a few months due to lack of evidence or some fucking shit to start again." After a puffing pause, he added, "And during this whole process, these dirty insects will enjoy some of our taxpayers' money. They deserve a bullet, not any fucking chance."

Vayu reached into his pocket, pulled out his mobile in a hurry and cast the bright beam of the mobile's torch on Abhimanyu's face.

"What the fuck are you doing?" Abhimanyu freaked out, frowning and covering his eyes.

Vayu's suspicion was right. "Sir, you are bleeding," Vayu informed, taking a closer look and ran toward the main road to bring the first aid box from their vehicle.

Abhimanyu was quite late in reaching the five-star hotel, Pebbles Pew. His massive metal wristwatch showed 2 p.m. Chaddha had rung his mobile several times since morning. That couldn't even crack the combined cloud of LSD, significant bleeding, the pain of those four stitches on his head, strong painkillers and sleep deprivation. He parked his Royal Enfield by the road outside the hotel's boundary wall as the local crowd and media gathered in front of the entrance. He looked at the peep-mirror of his bike to adjust the aviators on his nose.

"Shit!" he muttered, examining the blood-soaked bandage on his head.

"Good morning, Samim sir," one of the reporters in the crowd greeted as his mobile rang.

"Did he arrive?"

"Not yet," the reporter replied.

"Okay, taunt him about his late arrival and drug abuse. Make it big; it should become breaking news," Samim ordered over the phone.

The reporter assured Samim and put his mobile back into his pocket.

Abhimanyu felt a little dizzy under the blazing sun as he approached the entrance. A reporter rushed to him along with his cameraman instantly. The other reporters hastened to reach Abhimanyu like innumerable ants running towards a dead cockroach.

"DCP Abhimanyu, what's your opinion about Shanaya Mehta's death?" one of the reporters asked, almost shouting.

"No comments!" Abhimanyu answered, gently pushing a few reporters away to make his way to the hotel reception.

"Is it a normal death or murder or suicide?" Another reporter enquired.

Abhimanyu lost his patience a bit as they fenced him, leaving no way for him to walk any further. He raised his hand in the air to draw their attention and gestured at them to be quiet. He addressed the crowd loudly, "I haven't reached the crime scene yet. I can answer all your questions only if I know the complete scenario. So, please let me go and start my investigation. I will keep you updated."

The gathered crowd, microphones, big cameras and parked vans covered in media banners, equipped with antennas were enough to draw the attention of local groups and onlookers. That accumulative gathering almost blocked the traffic on the road and made chaos.

"Does that mean the police haven't even started investigation? It's been four hours since the incident was reported," Samim's appointed reporter darted a teasing question to get some reaction from Abhimanyu.

"No! The department has already started working on the case. I was a little caught up with other ongoing cases. Enough questions for now. Please let us work uninterruptedly," Abhimanyu managed to answer, trying hard to sustain his serenity.

"Another case or drugs kept you busy till now? What's your connection with the drug peddler, Chakra?" the same reporter asked. He was all set to push the correct buttons, which could tug the real Abhimanyu out of his shell of professionalism and get their desired sensational footage for high TRP.

Abhimanyu toughened his jaws, firmed his fists and whispered to himself, "Let it go!"

The same journalist teased again, "How did you get that wound on your head? Does that have anything do with your addiction?"

Abhimanyu rushed towards that journalist abruptly and blew a punch on his face, fracturing his nose. That journalist couldn't keep his balance against that powerful strike and fell on the people behind him, bleeding violently. All the camera lenses around started sucking that precious moment from every possible angle along with several flashes. The situation turned messier when Abhimanyu snatched one of the cameras, dashed it onto the ground and smashed it to pieces. The crowd started screaming and whistling.

Chaddha and Vayu rushed to the spot along with their police force. They had to scuffle with the crowd to reach Abhimanyu at the centre. Vayu grabbed Abhimanyu from behind and tried hard to lift his feet from the ground to overpower him. However, Abhimanyu's hefty muscles were bulky enough for Vayu to move him even an inch. Compelled by the situation, Vayu started dragging him away from the crowd in a hurry.

"It's Vayu, sir!" Vayu shouted, noticing Abhimanyu's attempt of swinging his elbow back. Vayu sighed as Abhimanyu gave up his fight, recognizing Vayu's voice from behind.

Chaddha and his men formed a human wall around the entrance of the hotel lawn and restricted the crowd. At the same time, Abhimanyu and Vayu managed to escape the chaos. They rushed towards the hotel reception, crossing that large, lavish green lawn and meticulously decorated garden of expensive trees in between.

"Welcome to Pebbles Pew, sir! Myself Rohan Agarwal, the manager of this hotel," a gallant man in perfectly ironed black suit, trousers and shining boots greeted them with a pleasant smile. His teeth and white shirt were immaculate.

"It's a pleasure that I got this opportunity to serve and assist you," the manager continued in his modulated voice and trained dialect.

Abhimanyu felt radically out of place after glancing over the surroundings. Everyone was in their best presentable form, perfectly attired. Not just the guests and staff at the hotel, even Vayu was looking fresh and energetic.

"Ridiculous!" Abhimanyu whispered, looking at his torn jeans, wrinkled white linen shirt, messy hair, a blood-soaked dirty bandage and unkempt beard.

"We are not here for our honeymoon. So cut your crap and take us to Shanaya's room," Abhimanyu snapped back, taking off his aviators.

Vayu sighed.

"Of course, sir! You can expect complete cooperation from our team," the manager replied more politely, demonstrating his management skill to his subordinates who were standing behind him and gestured Abhimanyu to follow him.

They passed the red-carpeted corridor which was decorated with expensive wooden furniture. The large oil paintings on the walls were illuminated under beamed lights. The ceilings were gilded and the gigantic ornate chandeliers were dripping with crystals.

"You should have ignored those reporters to avoid that chaos," Vayu suggested as they reached the lift lobby.

Abhimanyu stared angrily at him for a second and entered the elevator. Vayu and the manager followed him.

"Third floor, please!" The manager instructed the liftman as he looked at him for an order.

"Is she the same Shanaya Mehta who had won the Young Achiever's Award last year? One of her interviews was published in a business magazine," Abhimanyu enquired the manager, and after a thoughtful pause, he added, "Hmm...I don't remember the name of that magazine, though."

"Yes, sir! Mrs Shanaya Mehta, the CEO of Nischol Textile. She had to take over the business at a very young age after her father's death. It was just a factory then. Her hard work, dedication and intelligence built up this huge empire in just the last four years," the manager expressed his admiration.

"Oh shit! Another high-profile crap," Abhimanyu blabbered, sighing as they came out of the elevator, reaching the third floor. Vayu took a long breath looking at Abhimanyu.

"Doesn't she live in Noida?" Abhimanyu asked, frowning as they were crossing a similarly decorated corridor on the third floor. The manager nodded in affirmation.

"Then what the hell was she doing in this hotel?" Abhimanyu retorted.

"He means what was her purpose of staying in this hotel away from her home in the same city," Vayu sugar-coated. Abhimanyu exchanged a glance with him.

"One of her college friends, Jignesh Patel arranged her birthday party and a kind of reunion. He had booked ten suites for fifteen guests along with the swimming pool for the party. Jignesh Patel had paid in advance for all these bookings," the manager informed on the way to Shanaya Mehta's suite.

That luxurious suite had a master bedroom and a guest bedroom with attached bathrooms, a dining area, living room with couches, sofas and an LED smart television, guest powder room and a small bar counter. From fruit platters, assorted chocolates, nuts and cookies to a bottle of wine, no stone was left unturned in making the experience a truly memorable one.

Sub-inspector Dubey was busy with the forensic team, photographing every nook and corner of that suite.

"Dubey ji, what did I miss so far?" Abhimanyu asked, entering the suite.

"Nothing, sir! We haven't found anything that could lead us to any conclusion whether it's a murder or suicide or a natural death due to some health issues. Only post-mortem can tell," Dubey informed disappointingly.

"Let's look at the dead body," Vayu suggested.

Dubey led them to a spa-style master bathroom with deep-soaking Jacuzzi and sauna. Its white tiles on the walls and sky-blue ceiling created a calming effect with all the silvery and artistic plumbing appliances. It was so clean that initially they hesitated to step in with their dirty boots.

The corpse of Shanaya Mehta sank in the water inside the Jacuzzi. Though the foam on the water surface partially covered her naked torso, her breasts were exposed. Her long wavy hair touched the floor hanging outside the tub, arms resting on the handstands at either side of the container.

"There were no signs of forced entry. Moreover, the door was locked from inside. I have checked the CCTV. We haven't found anything suspicious in the entire suite; no bloodstain, no semen or saliva on the body, no damage to any property, no murder weapon, not even any foul smell. It seems like a ghost has killed her," Dubey informed as Vayu and Abhimanyu walked forth to take a closer look at the corpse.

She had an athletic body in her early forties; wide and slender shoulders, prominently defined bust, tapered torso which narrowed at the waist and widened again near the thighs. She lay in that tub like a finless mermaid.

"Let's send the dead body for autopsy then; we might get some breakthrough. And inform her family," Abhimanyu suggested, turning back to Dubey as if he was in a hurry to wrap up the case.

"Wait a minute!" Vayu interrupted, gesturing at one of the forensic experts to get him a pair of surgical gloves. He knelt by the tub and leaned over her face. "Have you checked the scalp thoroughly for any mark of needle or injection?" Vayu asked, wearing the gloves.

"Yes, we haven't found anything," the forensic expert replied. Vayu touched her face.

She was of fair complexion with sharp features. She had the kindest pair of coffee brown eyes trimmed by long gorgeous lashes. Her gentle eyes, which held a little warmth within them, were staring at the ceiling.

It was insanely beautiful – no mess, no bleeding, not even a single scratch, wound or bruise. Vayu stared at the craft of a crime, and felt like someone out there had challenged him – 'Play with me if you can!'

"Beautiful," Vayu whispered. Everyone in the room looked at him in shock.

"And what the fuck is that supposed to mean?" Abhimanyu sounded disgusted.

"Look inside the nostrils," Vayu whispered, lifting her nose by the thumb. "It's burnt inside... She inhaled some poison," he rejoined, examining the nostrils rigorously.

Everyone witnessed the sore area inside her nose, stumbling over Vayu's shoulders.

"Good job, Mr Backup! At least we have something to start with," Abhimanyu appreciated and ordered Dubey, "Comb the entire suite for any poison... got it?"

Dubey departed, nodding.

"Who found the dead body first?" Vayu asked as they reached the drawing-room.

"Sir, all of us actually. Mrs Shanaya Mehta asked us to wake her up early in the morning, around 6 a.m. and send her breakfast after an hour. So, I called on her mobile phone at around 5:45 a.m. She received the call, thanking me for waking her up on time. However, when one of our men rang the doorbell to serve breakfast an hour later, she didn't open the door. He came back after fifteen minutes, but the result was the same. When we couldn't reach her, we had to use our duplicate key," the manager informed.

"Did she mention any reason for waking up early? After the late-night party, she must have been tired," Vayu enquired, trying to reach some conclusion.

"Yes, she had to catch a flight to Mumbai."

"Hmm… it's a murder in that case," Vayu concluded and continued after a pause, "The poison in her nostril has already crossed out the possibility of natural death and this early morning flight has knocked off the possibility of suicide as nobody would plan for suicide and catch a flight at the same time."

"That leaves us with one option," Abhimanyu muttered thoughtfully and added softly, "homicide."

Everyone became silent for a few moments before Vayu said, "I don't think we will find any murder weapon here."

"Why?" Abhimanyu asked.

"Our unsub is organized and smart. Nothing happened inside this suite except the death. As you can see, there is no sign of struggle or protest. It was as smooth as a hot knife slicing through butter," Vayu explained as they returned to the corridor.

Abhimanyu nodded, comprehending and mumbled softly, "But, we have to complete that routine."

"What's unsub?" the manager asked hesitatingly.

"Unidentified subject," Abhimanyu and Vayu replied in unison exchanging glances. They realize their mistake of discussing a homicide case in front of a person who was not a part of their investigation team.

In the meanwhile, Chaddha arrived, panting. "Sir, everything is in control down there; no more crowd outside," he almost shouted, pulling a hankie out of his pocket. Then, he moved closer to Abhimanyu, wiping the sweats on his face and whispered, "But some reporters aren't easy to get rid of. They might show something against you on their channels or do something more."

Abhimanyu chuckled before ordering Chaddha to scrutinize all the CCTV footages.

"I need a list of all your guests along with their contact details. And none of them can leave this building until my next order," Abhimanyu ordered the manager while Chaddha departed, tagging along with one of the hotel's security guards.

"I am scared that I might fail to obey this particular order," the manager denied politely.

Abhimanyu pointed his finger at him and was about to shout, but the manager started again in his modulated tone, "Sir, please try to understand, all our guests are highly respected, reputable, powerful and influential people of our country. It will jeopardize my career and business."

Before Abhimanyu's ego and anger took the shape of the Hulk, Vayu interfered, "Okay, at least give them a heads up that they might have to turn up if our investigation demands. And gather all those fifteen guests who had attended the party last night."

"Sure, sir! I will gather all of them in the assembly hall," the manager assured with a pleasant smile. Abhimanyu glowered at Vayu as the manager departed.

"Sir, even if we ignore the fact of influence and whatever that manager said, it's not feasible for us to interrogate all the guests of this huge building in a single day," Vayu explained. Abhimanyu sighed in agreement, reluctantly.

"So, what do you think? How did your organized unsub do it?" Abhimanyu teased as they approached the assembly hall where Shanaya's guests were waiting for them.

Vayu nodded, making a clueless face followed by a soft mumble, "I am certain about one thing, though. That suite isn't our crime scene."

"What do you mean? Your organized unsub killed her somewhere else and then placed the dead body here? That's not possible, Mr Backup! The door was locked from inside, and Dubey ji has already confirmed that from the CCTV," Abhimanyu retorted, and Vayu had no answer for him. "The manager unlocked the door in front of many people. And they checked that the door was locked from the inside," Abhimanyu continued till they reached the assembly hall.

"Let's see if Shanaya's guests can get us some clue," Vayu replied, glancing over those fifteen faces gathered in the hall.

It felt like a viva voce, where fifteen students were eagerly waiting for their turn to face the external examiners. They were standing in a row, stressed and nervous, except one lady in a blue saree. She looked quite thrilled, basking the suspense of the circumstances like a studious girl who had finished the syllabus in advance, and was prepared to show off her knowledge to her classmates.

Abhimanyu and Vayu settled themselves on a large couch, following the warm gesture from the manager. A pair of coffee mugs, packed water bottles, notepads and pens were perfectly arranged on a glass-topped, low-height table in front of the couch with a single chair facing the sofa.

"Sir, these are their names, occupations, contacts and other details," the manager said, handing over a sheet to Abhimanyu. "I will be right outside the hall if you need anything else," he added with a smile. He left after Abhimanyu nodded, impressed at the neatly-done job.

"Mr Backup, I want you to lead the investigation," Abhimanyu said.

"Jignesh Patel," Vayu called the first name from the list.

A tall, fair and lean man in a sky-blue summer suit donned over a bright white shirt tucked in a skinny, tapered khaki trousers came forward with the rhythmical noise of his shiny, ponied boots. He lounged himself on that single chair, crossed his leg and laid one of his hands on the chair's backrest. He had a thin and long face with a beaked nose hanging over his mouth;

a thick-framed spectacle covered his deep-set eyes, flattened cheekbones and stretched lips.

"Your name?" Vayu asked, keeping his mobile on the table, recording their investigation.

He opened his mouth spilling a heavy Gujarati accent. "Come on! You called a name, and I have come forward responding to your call, right?"

Vayu smiled at the predictability of human behaviours. Profiling, a branch of forensics that literally offers a sneak-peek into an individual's mind, was Vayu's specialization after IPS, and this was his first opportunity to implement his research and study in real. Predicting Jignesh's Gujarati accent was not rocket science, but Vayu was happy about his first baby step of profiling – predicting pronunciation and origin based on mere surnames.

The concept of analysing the psyche of the offender could help to predict future offenses and victims. In present times, profiling is vastly applied in the USA and few other countries for predictive identification of suspects by establishing common patterns of behaviour, and comparing them with the behavioural analysis of successfully closed cases in the past.

Profiling was introduced in India at an experimental level. Few selected IPS toppers got the opportunity to study behavioural science, and Vayu was one of them.

"Hey hero, just answer! You are not here to question us," Abhimanyu admonished Jignesh, toughening his jaws.

"Jignesh Patel," he answered reluctantly, pretending a laidback attitude to hide his racing heart.

"How did you know Mrs Shanaya Mehta?" Vayu asked, reading something on his mobile.

"We studied in the same college. Not only me, but all of us here were batch-mates in Indian Statistical Institute." Jignesh seemed much relaxed while answering.

The Sinful Silence • 23

Vayu observed the laughter lines around Jignesh's eyes. They were in just the right amount. He must be a happy person, but at that moment, he was deadly serious.

"So, do you guys often arrange this kind of reunion? Are you guys in continuous touch?" Abhimanyu interfered.

"No, I just bumped into Shanaya a few days back on social media, and we started chatting a bit. Then gradually, in some casual conversations, this reunion plan came up and we decided to arrange this event on the occasion of her birthday," Jignesh said, demonstrating his devil-may-care attitude. He adjusted himself on his chair to lay his back, seeking more comfort.

Vayu still remembered that Skype conference where one of the high profilers from the FBI advised them to focus on observations. India had no prior behavioural analysis database to refer to which is why observation is the critical skill to predict and define an Indian pattern of crime.

Look at that big show-off, Vayu thought while observing Jignesh. He kept his hand hanging over the chair's backrest, so that no one could evade that glossy Rolex around his wrist and Brioni tag on the cuff of his suit. His crossed-leg posture exposed the bottom of one of his herringbone textured boots to exhibit the carved Jimmy Choo. His frequent adjustment of the spectacles was just an excuses to flaunt the Moscot frame.

According to Vayu's studies and researches, every human behaviour and habit is triggered by some emotions or incidents. There are many reasons why a person may become flamboyant, but insecurities and childhood experiences of rejection are the two most common reasons amongst them. A man only shows off when he thinks that others don't consider him worthy or some puerile incidents make him believe that he is worthless.

Vayu found Jignesh an ideal case, a combination of both deep-seated insecurities and childhood rejections, after reading one of Jignesh's interviews on different websites in that short period. Jignesh was the owner of a newly-established stock agency in Mumbai, doing quite fascinating business for three years as he started his career as a mere broker. A pleasant smile lit up Vayu's face as he could confidently assume that Jignesh had arranged that reunion to show-off his newly achieved empire and abundant wealth. 'But what is that incident which made these fifteen people so special to you? Why are you so desperate to win their respect?' Vayu thought loudly enough to whisper.

"Tell me about the incident that has been haunting you since you have passed out of your college," Vayu asked impulsively. Abhimanyu exchanged a glance with Vayu in shock as he had no clue about the relevance of that question.

"Wh... What incident? There is no such incident... haunting and fuck," Jignesh stammered. He pulled a hankie out of his pocket to wipe the sweat off.

"Sweating in an air-conditioned room is not a good indication of health, Mr Patel," Vayu said, offering him one of their water bottles. Jignesh grabbed the bottle and gulped down the water, his hands shaking.

"Let me help you," Vayu continued. "You are a self-made man, coming from a poor background, having no reference or influence. You have earned immense respect and money in the stock market. Starting as a mere broker, you have built your own stock agency because of your hard work, grand vision, dedication and marketing skill. However, your friends were not aware of this avatar of Jignesh Patel. So, you returned among them to earn their respect, to see envy in their eyes, and establish your superiority." Vayu paused for a moment while observing the minute wrinkles on Jignesh's face, which suggested his affirmation and pride.

"But why is their approval of your success so important to you?" Vayu asked while Abhimanyu was a mute spectator, as if he was witnessing a wizard perform a spellbinding act. "See, if you won't tell us the truth, your friends will tell their versions of the story, which might lead our investigation against you. This is your chance to tell us yourself," Vayu advised, pretending to be his well-wisher.

"Yes, I always wanted to show them who I am today because they always humiliated me for my poverty and lean body. I tried hard to win this group's hearts, to be one of them, but they always treated me like a piece of shit. I had to spend my entire college life alone and isolated. These motherfuckers have never been my friends. Yesterday, I showed them my lifestyle. I paid for them to live one day of my life, what they can't even dare to dream about," Jignesh said calmly under his breath, occasionally gnashing his teeth.

"But unfortunately, you stumbled upon the fact that Shanaya Mehta is always more successful and wealthy. You couldn't digest that failure even after so many years of your efforts and planned to kill her," Abhimanyu interfered, provoking Jignesh's disgust and anger.

Jignesh chuckled and muttered a soft 'No'. "I have had no grudges against her. She was just immature and had a bad taste in choosing people. But unlike these morons, she never humiliated or insulted me. Rather, she always admired my intelligence, punctuality and brilliance. By the way, I was one of the toppers in my batch and used to help her in studies," Jignesh continued in a low voice, slowly plucking the leaves of his memory.

"She was bright, eloquent, smart and charismatic but unfocused, disturbed and self-destructive at the same time. Otherwise, she would have been the topper every year," Jignesh said, inattentively playing with his watch.

The slightest stretch of Jignesh's laughter line under his eyes, couldn't escape Vayu's attention. 'Look at that blush he fails to hide,' Vayu's mind whispered.

"So, whom did she choose over you?" Vayu darted his next question based on his observation.

"Excuse me!" Jignesh looked quite uncomfortable.

"She rejected your romantic proposal and chose someone among these fourteen people. Who's that?" Vayu reframed his query, sipping his coffee.

"Rizwan," Jignesh answered. His eyes glowered as he said, "See, this murder has nothing to do with that rejection. Shanaya was the most popular girl in our batch. The sweetheart of all these guys' secret desires and the reason for most of the girls' jealousy. I just took advantage of her birthday to secure everyone's presence, you know. Otherwise... none of them would have come... you know."

"I am done. Sir, you can ask if you have any questions," Vayu finished, jotting down something on his pad.

"You may go as of now, Mr Jignesh. Don't leave the city without our permission," Abhimanyu said authoritatively.

"One last question; are you married?" Vayu enquired. Jignesh shook his head in negative.

Jignesh stood there for a few seconds. Abhimanyu and Vayu stared at him until he whispered, "I think Rizwan Ahmed is the man you are looking for."

They exchanged glances as Jignesh departed.

"What was that? Are you some kind of a psychic?" Abhimanyu wondered.

Vayu laughed briefly before answering, "No, that was just a calculative guess based on keen observations of his expressions and gestures."

"Huh! Profiling... Good job, Mr Backup!"

Abhimanyu's phone rang and he pulled it out from his pocket. He glanced over the screen and walked towards the exit. In the meanwhile, Vayu had stolen a glance at his screen to read the caller's name – Chakra. Abhimanyu had a short conversation with Chakra over the phone as he stood near the door, little away from the couch as Vayu waited there for his return.

"Mr Backup, it's time for you to really back me up. I must leave for an important job. You lead the interrogation and keep me updated about the progress. I will ask Chaddha to assist you," Abhimanyu instructed returning to Vayu, and rushed back towards the exit before Vayu could say anything.

Vayu looked at Abhimanyu leaving the hall, thinking, 'Look at this addict running like a thirsty man to the mirage of a puddle in an oasis.' He wondered how a DCP could neglect the homicide of a business tycoon, which will hit the headlines of all national newspapers the next morning. How could a man like Abhimanyu become a DCP? He was so impatient, unfocused, hostile, short-tempered and rude. Vayu sighed heavily and read the next name on the list – Juhi Srivastava.

"Sir ji, there is something you must see in the CCTV footage," Chaddha announced as he entered the hall carrying a laptop in his hands.

After scrutinizing the CCTV footage several times, Vayu asked, "Isn't that man, the third one from the left?" Vayu's eyes pointed to a tall man with an athletic build among those fourteen guests who waiting for their turn. Chaddha nodded, confirming.

The footage showed a suited, short-haired man helping Shanaya lurch towards her suite as he wrapped his left arm around her waist, and her right arm was hanging around his shoulder. She rested her body weight on his arms as it seemed her feet had no strength left to bear her own weight. The man used his right hand to unlock the door and somehow, they managed to enter the suite, stumbling. The man walked away through the corridor as the door closed from inside, after a few minutes. The clock on the screen ticked away several hours without any significant incident; only a few employees of the hotel passed through the corridor. Vayu fast-forwarded the footage until a man in hotel uniform arrived there, pushing a large breakfast and beverage trolley. He rang the doorbell, waiting there for a few moments before ringing it again. He repeated his attempts to seek the attention of the occupant and rushed through the corridor, leaving the trolley in front of the door. Few more minutes ticked away before that man returned, along with the manager and a few others.

Vayu paused the clip and mumbled thoughtfully, "Rizwan Ahmed!"

"Have you already interrogated him? Did he mention this?" Chaddha asked in a hurry to jump to a conclusion. Vayu shook his head.

"Then, how do you know this man in the video is Rizwan?" Not getting any response from Vayu, Chaddha concluded, "Oh! The manager introduced them to you?"

"No! The broken-hearted, one-sided lover Jignesh told us that Shanaya had chosen someone from this group over him. Rizwan Ahmed should be our prime suspect," Vayu told inattentively, noting down the timestamps from the CCTV footage. "The most popular, charismatic and attractive girl in the group of college students is likely to fall for the most handsome guy in the group; sounds stereotypical but happens most of the time," Vayu continued in a low voice, focusing on the screen. "Connect all the dots and you will get the name of that most handsome man, third from the left."

Chaddha pondered, linking the dots, and said, "Hmm!"

"This footage just says Shanaya was weak enough to walk. The reason could be overconsumption of alcohol in the party or common health issues, or poison, and Rizwan helped her to reach her suite," Vayu said, sighing.

"Moreover, she made a call to the reception after she had reached the suite to wake her up in the morning. So, whatever might be the reason for her weakness, it was jiffy; must be light faintness or something," Chaddha contributed through his observation.

Shanaya's birthday party was like a social gathering and a reunion of old college friends who were an integral part of each other's lives several years back. The friends who used to share food from the same plate in the college canteen. They had now gathered to celebrate exotic cuisines, expensive wines and gleesome moments.

A hint of smile waved on Vayu's lips as he visualized that jovial ambience – the partners in crimes of college life burst into laughter in each other's arms on a stupid joke. When they giggled on that old rumours about some professors, stole a few glances of their long faded crushes, and danced to the latest tunes, forgetting the harsh reality of their lives for that moment.

However, there was one sullen face among them, hidden beneath a happy mask, a loud groan suppressed under their laughter. An unhealed wound which was never healed and bled that day freshly. An old trusted hand which carried poison instead of a birthday gift and a mind which knitted the brutal and untraceable plan.

"Who are you?" Vayu whispered to himself.

"Sorry, sir?" Chaddha asked as he faintly overheard Vayu's whisper.

"Someone might have poisoned her in the party, probably a slow-poison which would give our unsub ample time to arrange some alibis to prove his or her innocence. Only the post-mortem report can tell us the nature of that poison. When are we getting the report?"

"In a week or two. Normally, it takes more than a month. However, the forensic department has expedited the process by looking at the department's mounting pressure with each passing hour. Shanaya was one of the biggest financial supporters of the ruling party," Chaddha informed.

"But I wonder whether our boss cares about any pressure," Vayu said mockingly and added after chuckling, "He is carefree enough to leave the investigation in the middle to meet that drug peddler, Chakra."

"Let's move to the next guest," Chaddha chose to evade the topic.

The city had just glided into the darkness of late evening, wiping off the faint brightness from the sky. The air became colder, being deprived of the scorching touch of the sun.

Oorja caressed the goosebumps on her bare neck, shoulders and upper arms, staring at the dark silhouette of the woods at the horizon as a cool, capricious breeze sneaked into her motel room though that tiny window. The highway by that motel was freshly built. A perfectly painted yellow line on the black and shiny road seemed unreal, like a kid's painting. Oorja moved closer to the window as a car slowed down in front of the motel. A pleasing smile lit her face expecting her man in that car. However, that car went away after a tiny halt, leaving her sighing disappointingly.

Oorja had introduced him to the syndicate a year ago, but never got a chance to meet him personally until last month when he arrived at her flat at midnight. That night was still vivid in her mind – that long conversation over wine, those lingering stares, those excuses to lay hands on each other. He had tugged her abruptly, grabbing her waist and pressed her against his toughened torso. She felt his defined chest as her breast had squeezed against him. She had caught the back of his head, pulled him close and nibbled his lower lips.

This young, intelligent, smart and attractive lady was the syndicate's communication device. Oorja was responsible for finding new recruits suitable for any specific task. She was the messenger between the members who had no common channel to be acquainted with each other apart from being a member of the syndicate. She posed as a social worker for the outside world, but had started her career of crime as a con artist at an early age due to the desperate need for money. Her acting skill, perfect pronunciation in seven different languages, innocent appearance and the ability to mingle in any surroundings made her invincible. She had no mobile phone, credit card, driving license, pan card, bank account or any document or device which could track her activity, except for a voter card with the address of her village. Her mode of communications were public telephone booths or meetings in-person.

She was like the thread that holds all the flowers together to form a garland, but remains invisible from outside. She had been living the life of a ghost since she had joined the syndicate.

A couple of sharp thuds on the door startled Oorja. She rushed towards the door, anticipating her desired man at the door. She looked through the peephole on the door to get a glimpse of her visitor. But she could only see the shut door of the room on the opposite side. She was reluctant to open the door as that cheap motel by the highway was quite unsafe for a lone female. She was irritated that he had chosen this place. She had demanded an adventurous and thrilling date, not a risky one. Her invisible visitor banged the door once again.

"Who...who is it?" Oorja asked, fumbling.

"Room service, madam," a husky voice answered, which comforted her a bit.

She could gather her courage to reply, "I don't need any kind of service now. Just leave me alone and don't disturb."

"It's a scheduled maintenance activity to keep all the rooms clean for our clients, ma'am. I might lose my job if I don't obey my manager."

Oorja wondered whether she had heard that voice before. Curiosity got the better of her to open the door partly and peep through it to catch a glimpse of him. Before she could comprehend anything, a nippy and violent thrust on the door knocked her down on the floor. The man rushed into the room and latched the door.

"Don't... don't even think that I am a helpless, lone and an innocent prey," Oorja fumbled, crawling backward and groping on the floor to find something handy to fight back.

That tall, wide and muscular intruder hastened to her and kneeled on the floor. Behind the monkey cap, Oorja couldn't see anything other than his eyes, which failed to conceal the seething vengeance beneath the layer of mischievousness. He held her head tightly on the floor, grabbing her mouth while she shouted for help. Her eyes rolled up in suffocation. She could smell his surgical glove. She used both her hands to get rid of his large, thick and firm palm over her mouth, but failed to move it even an inch. She regretted having taken off her heels to comfort her feet as her feeble barefoot kicks were not helping.

He had locked her legs underneath his heavy torso and pulled out a polythene sheet from his black overcoat. He threw that sheet open; it spread over the floor untidily. He got down and started dragging her to place her in the middle of that polythene sheet. She put up a fight. His grip on her mouth loosened up in that hustle to let her scream for help again. He placed his palm back on her mouth before she could blink further and pulled out a knife from his overcoat. He inserted the tip of his knife into her cleavage, keeping the sharper edge away from her skin, and tugged the knife to rip apart her dress till her waist. Oorja realized that her voice was not reaching anyone. She decided to see the monster's face before giving up; at least she would have something to avenge for if she survived that night. She stretched her hand out and snatched the monkey cap. To her immense surprise, the man helped her remove the cap while it was stuck over his neck.

"What…What that fuck! Abhimanyu," Oorja screamed. Her lips quivered, tears rolled down her cheeks and her face had turned red.

"You are a spoilsport," Abhimanyu said disappointingly, releasing her from his grasp and lying down next to her.

They lay there panting and gazing at that sluggish ceiling fan for few more moments before Oorja broke the silence and, "So, this was your surprise role play?"

They exchanged a glance smiling; an overwhelming relief was vivid on Oorja's face.

She rolled towards him, rested her head on his chest. "I had almost forgotten. What did you name this shit?" Abhimanyu laughed as she said, "Billionaire bitch and a contract killer. Oh god!" Oorja giggled unbuttoning Abhimanyu's shirt.

"And why the hell will the billionaire bitch check-in at such a cheap hotel?" she asked, helping him to take off his overcoat and shirt.

"Those five-star hotels are highly secured; no one would have allowed me to cross even the reception in this get-up," he said, stroking the bulgy portion of her breasts.

"Ahh... and why... why do we need this huge polythene sheet, overcoat and surgical gloves?" she asked in a quivering voice, enjoying the touch of his rough and strong palm.

"Those are the props; a proper prop always makes the role play intense. An experienced contract killer never leaves any trace behind; no witness, not even any tiniest part of his existence," he answered, freeing her breast from the shackle of her silky bandeau and caressed her with his face.

She rode on him, followed by a lopsided smile, grabbed one of his hands to guide it inside her lingerie, and whispered, "Kill me then and don't leave any trace!"

He raised himself on the floor with the support of his other hand and gently bit her upper lip. Her nails scratched his collar muscles. She made her tongue busy inside his mouth, brushing his teeth, palate and tongue. His fingers brushed over the thatch of hair inside her lingerie before pushing one of his fingers into the slick, hot core. She moaned in pleasure, fumbling over his belt buckle as she hurried to take his jeans off.

"I will kill you, but you need to help me before that," Abhimanyu whispered as he freed his lips for a moment.

Oorja opened his belt and reached for his zip, nodding.

"I need the names and whereabouts of those two men," Abhimanyu demanded, grabbing her busy hand, which had slipped inside his underwear, defeating the zip.

The Sinful Silence • 35

"Now, you are being the spoilsport. Don't ruin this moment. You can't imagine how horny I am right now," she whispered, occasionally gnashing and attempting to snatch her hand with a jerk from his grasp. He released her hand.

"Some probable consequences of that night are haunting me all the time. I can't afford to spoil even a second while I am with a nymph, but my mind is restless. Those two men might spoil my whole career. I had taken a huge risk and sacrificed the love of life," he said, cupping her face and planting kisses.

"Okay!" she almost screamed in frustration, pushing him away. She got down on the floor from his lap and started sullenly, "See, I had been ordered to find two men who were desperate to kill for money. They had to have a weak financial and social background and must be non-residents of Noida. Basically, two scapegoats that could easily be immolated after the task."

"Hmm... Yusuf Malik and Suraj Kumar, as I can remember their names," she added after a thoughtful delay. She continued, "Both of them are from Jasana, a small village of Faridabad district. They had come to Noida for work. Yusuf is a plumber and Suraj is a truck driver."

"Where can I find them?" he asked, drawing a pouch of cocaine from his pocket, pouring a few pinches of powder on that polythene sheet.

She guffawed for a few moments and said, "This powder has literally fucked your brain, man. Are you crazy? Aren't you supposed to know that? You were assigned to take care of this job."

"Yes, and I had assured them that I can handle it all by myself," he said, segregating the tiny pile of powder in two thin lines. "Why the fuck did they have to summon those two jokers?" he said, clenching his jaws and snorting those thin white stripes bending forward.

"They were not confident. After all, Ahi was your fiancée," she answered, caressing his hair.

He raised his head and glanced at the ceiling, breathing deeply. He rubbed his thumb around his nose to wipe the scattered cocaine and said, "If they spill out any name, mine will be the first."

"Don't worry! The syndicate has already triggered a search operation to chop off those loose ends. However, they couldn't manage any lead except the confirmation that they are still in Noida," she informed to console him, gazing at his restless and flickering eyes.

"I can't afford to jeopardize my life and career because of syndicate's stupid decision. Who gave the order?" he murmured softly.

"It was discussed in a meeting and decided by all the members of the group, except Chakra. He argued against the decision of killing her and suggested an alternative of destroying the manuscript. But they were not ready to take any risk by leaving Ahi alive."

An eerie silence conquered the room until Oorja said, "I have their pictures in my room. You can keep them if that helps you find them."

Abhimanyu nibbled her earlobe and whispered, "Thanks!"

"A...Are you plann..." she fumbled in pleasing surprise. Before she could finish her words, she felt Abhimanyu's long and strong gloved fingers tightened around her throat, cutting off the air supply. She tried to pry his fingers away, but slowly she was losing consciousness. She swatted at his hand in desperation for breathing, but his grip was too strong to wriggle out of. Her sharp nails scratched his hand's skin and made him moan mutedly in pain, but he kept on squeezing her throat. Her protest became weaker as time passed. Her eyes bulged out, mouth fell open, and her face turned red.

The Sinful Silence • 37

Abhimanyu felt a strange numbness in his arms. His grasp on Oorja's throat became feeble as he couldn't gather his strength back. He heard a whisper in his mind, 'You are not a monster.' Oorja grabbed his wrists, pushed them away, and gulped a lungful of air.

It was too late for Abhimanyu to think of any alternative. He was left with no option but to kill Oorja. Abhimanyu closed his eyes to refrain himself from watching Oorja's suffering, ignored all the voices in his mind, and tightened his grasp again.

Oorja struggled for a few more moments against his firm grip before giving up forever. Her lifeless body collapsed on that polythene sheet as he released her.

Vayu and Chaddha had managed to interrogate twelve of Shanaya's guests till the manager requested they break for dinner. Most of the guests returned to their rooms, except Rizwan Ahmed and that lady who had been sustaining her enthusiasm since afternoon to tell a hell lot of secrets of her college-mates.

"Shanaya's husband and sister have arrived at the morgue. We had to postpone the autopsy because we had to wait for them," Dubey informed as they returned to the assembly hall after finishing their dinner.

"Hmm... otherwise, media will get another chance to blame us. Especially after Abhimanyu's behaviour towards them, they will look for every possible opportunity to strip us in front of the masses," Vayu said, settling on the couch.

"Brutal police rip Shanaya's body before her loved ones can see her for the last time," Chaddha said dramatically. Then after a large burp, he added, "Oh! The food was really good."

Vayu and Dubey stared at him. "That might be the headline, you know," Chaddha said.

"Would you like to call them here for questioning?" Dubey asked, laughing at Chaddha.

"No! I would like to visit them at their home. I have to explore Shanaya's home," Vayu denied and thoughtfully added. "A home says a lot, even about things its inhabitants are not aware of."

Dubey left to carry out the orders.

Eleven of the twelve interrogated guests, except for Jignesh, had mentioned about a heated fight between Jignesh and Rizwan, followed by a scuffle between them. Shanaya intervened to bring sanity; few of their friends stepped forward to help her. Though they refrained from fighting, their tiff continued. Finally, Shanaya had slapped Rizwan while raising the ages-old topic of Shanaya's rejection of Jignesh's proposal. Rizwan left the party for a couple of hours after that muddle until Shanaya called and pleaded him to join before the cake-cutting ceremony.

"Sachidananda Mishra is my name," the next witness said.

Vayu and Chaddha exchanged a glance on hearing his name, as it was awkwardly contrasting with his appearance. He had a trendy haircut, pierced eyebrow ring and a pointed beard that traced the jaw line paired with a floating moustache. The tattoos on his forearms, throat and neck were peeping outside his blue Henley neck T-shirt, scruffily tugged inside his tapered khaki trousers.

"But I like to go by the name, Sa… Sandy," Sachidananda fumbled.

Chaddha chortled and picked up the glass of water from the centre table to avoid any eye-contact with Vayu or Sandy. Sandy kept staring at him; humiliation vivid in his eyes.

"What do you do for a living, Sandy?" Vayu enquired.

"I am an an… animation artist; a free… freelancer." His stammering increased, making it difficult for him to complete the sentence.

It wasn't difficult for Vayu to read that Sandy couldn't control his anger, especially when triggered by humiliation. And an angry man spills out more truth than a stable mind is capable of hiding.

"So, basically, you are jobless, if I am not wrong." Vayu pressed on his wound

"I cho...cho...choose not to be a...a...a slave. I work when I...I...wish to. I am an artist and not a slave of money," Sandy almost shrieked.

Vayu kept gazing at him, wearing a humiliating smirk.

"Listen, I...I don't give a fuck to this party, co...college friends, Shanaya's b...birthday or any fu...fucking things here, you know. I...I have nothing do with her de...death. This Jig...Jig...Jignesh insisted me to join. I had re...re...reached out to him for some money a few months ba...ba...back. He said that this party is an op...op...opportunity for me to fetch some in...in...investment from Shanaya. She is filthy rich, you know and has a hell lot of in...in...influence in the market. Anyway, she re...re...refused to help me," he continued in one breath, stammering.

"Not a slave of money, is it?" Vayu mocked in a low voice.

"Yes, I am not! I just want people to appreciate my art, and I need money for my art," Sandy said in a steady voice, without a single fumble. "Neither, I...I couldn't crack any in...interview to get a job which could ba...ba...back my art financially, nor I could con...convince any producer," he concluded in a low voice as he vented his anger a bit.

"Is it an animation movie you are trying to create?" Vayu asked, offering him a glass of water. He gulped down the water in a hurry and nodded in affirmation.

"I need a studio, a hell lot of expensive devices, and few people to complete my project. Shanaya was my last hope," he said without stumbling on any word.

Vayu noticed that Sandy didn't stammer when he spoke about his project. "Interesting!" he whispered, grasping Sandy's unspoken words. His old-fashioned name suggested that he had been raised by an orthodox, theist and Hindu parent, poor enough to support their son's dream. They might have shackled his freedom of expression, smashed his confidence, and forced him to manage a job to secure his future. Their lives had taught them that mediocrity is the only surviving weapon for the underprivileged.

However, it was obvious to Vayu that Sandy couldn't give up his dream. And his efforts of blotting out his true self might have triggered his stammering. As soon as he could shrug off his parents' dependency, he started creating a personality in the core of his mind, the personality he always dreamt off – Sandy. Sandy was a smart, confident and a stylish animation artist who didn't stammer. Vayu wondered whether another character was hiding beneath some drape of his creative mind who couldn't tolerate that Shanaya had refused to help Sandy and hence, he murdered her.

"What do you think? What might be the reason that Shanaya didn't show interest in your project?" Vayu enquired.

"Lack of kno…knowledge! That bitch had no….no…. no sense of art; money-minded cap…capitalist," he replied in disgust.

"I see. But Shanaya could have just donated you the money. I have read that she used to do a lot of charity to NGOs and small entrepreneurs. After all, you are one of her close friends, and she was filthy rich, right?" Vayu retorted to find and squeeze the wound which would make Sandy tell the truth in pain.

"How am I…I…I…I supposed to know that? It's her… her…her money her…her wish; the bloody whore!" Sandy said in irritation. The wrinkles on his face expressed a bottomless disgust.

Vayu felt like hitting the jackpot when he heard the word 'whore'. He was certain that mere rejection of funding couldn't trigger such a strong word; there must be some secret behind that.

"Whore! Why?" Vayu asked in a spontaneous reaction.

"Nothing…I…I…I just bawled that out in…in…in anger," he responded in a desperate attempt to generalize the conversation. However, the tiny bite on his own tip of the tongue couldn't evade Vayu's observation.

"Anger!" Vayu echoed with a mellow smile and said, "So much anger that could drive you to kill her, like it made you slip your tongue."

"Come on! You...you...you are just in a hurry to...to...to close the case by framing the weakest person in your suspect pool who can...can...cannot fight back," he complained, frowning.

"Are you married?" Vayu asked immediately after he finished.

"No."

Vayu laughed and told, "You may leave as of now and don't leave the city without our permission."

Abhimanyu stumbled on his trembling feet as he entered the elevator and had to grab the door of the elevator to stop himself from falling on the floor. He fumbled on the switchboard to find the right button for his floor. He took a couple of seconds to realize that he was not alone. A woman and a little girl huddled in the farthest corner, terrified. The girl hid behind the woman as Abhimanyu smiled at her. The woman was trying hard to behave normally, but her restless eyeballs were eloquent enough to showcase her fright. In between her gaze to find her floor number on the digital display inside the elevator, she was stealing a few glimpses at Abhimanyu. And each of her glances just raised her heartbeats. The blood-soaked bandage on his head, the messy hair, the bleeding hand, the shaky feet, and inebriated activities scared her.

"It has to be a boy," Ahi said, resting her head on Abhimanyu's bare chest as they savoured some leisure moments on the bed after having sex. She dragged herself on him to reach his face and whispered, followed by a passionate kiss, "Exactly like you."

"No way! It must be a girl with the same eyes as you; bluish-green, fairylike, and hypnotic." He kissed her eyes one by one.

The Sinful Silence • 43

The computerized female voice of the elevator tugged him out from the pondering state of his mind, which was lost in the maze of Ahi's memory as it announced the arrival of the fifth floor. The woman sped out of the elevator immediately after the door opened, tugging along the kid with her. He stood there like a mannequin till the door opened on the ninth floor, and he started lurching towards his flat.

"Rizwan Ahmed," the man in blue shorts and white T-shirt answered Vayu's usual warm-up question after finishing a whole bottle of water in few non-stop gulps. He had the kind of face that could stop females in their tracks. Vayu guessed he must be used to that, the sudden pause in a woman's natural expression when they looked his way followed by overcompensating with a nonchalant gaze and a weak smile. He had brownish complexion. His decently trimmed short hair made his chiselled face sharper. The popped-up cheekbone, sharp and short nose, well-defined jaw line and thin lips gave him a skeletal look. His salt and pepper stubble honed his rough and tough appearance. His muscular torso was at war to tear off his T-shirt. His muscles rippled across his body, along with numerous veins that spread over his arms bulging beneath his skin.

"*Aur chahiye?*" Chaddha asked, offering another bottle.

Rizwan waved his palm, refusing Chaddha and said, "No, thanks!" after a loud burp.

"What do you do for a living?" Vayu asked as Rizwan settled.

"I work in a sports-club as a fitness trainer. But sometimes, I do train personally at home as well, specifically for those clients who can't attend my regular sessions," Rizwan replied plainly. "But I charge extra from them," he added with a laugh.

"What's the name of your club?" Chaddha intervened.

"G.K. Sports & Fitness. It's in sector 50." Rizwan had a strange calmness that Vayu hadn't seen before. How could he be so composed, especially when he was being interrogated in a murder investigation?

"You must visit our club sometimes, sir," Rizwan advised Chaddha. "Just attend few of our demo sessions. I am sure you will find immense interest in fitness; it will change your life," he continued enthusiastically. It seemed that Rizwan had a habit of convincing unfit people to attend his sessions.

Vayu had a glance at Chaddha's bulgy tummy, peeping at them through the gaps between the buttons of his uniform and said, "Yeah, you must try."

Chaddha found himself in an awkward situation. He giggled and said, "*Kya* sir, *aap bhi*!"

"How did you know Mrs Shanaya Mehta?" Vayu inquired, leaning closer to Rizwan to read every minute wrinkle on his face.

"Friend, a close college friend." Rizwan's hands, earlier casually resting on his lap, traversed to his face and rubbed his stubble. As if someone had thrown a pebble in a tranquil lake to create ripples.

Humans have no control over their hand gestures while speaking; it's natural and inevitable human behaviour. Rizwan's stubble rubbing was the unintentional indication of his lie or half-truth. It was not hard for Vayu to see that Rizwan was pretending to be calm.

Vayu smiled and said, "That's it?"

"But we have heard something else," Chaddha interfered. "Will you tell us the truth by yourself, or should I help you?"

The permanent jovial expression on Chaddha's double-chinned, large and soft face had evaporated. Vayu was certain that Chaddha hadn't taken Rizwan's fitness advice positively. Vayu glanced at Chaddha.

"I meant, we had a close relation in our college days. A little more than friendship. However, we had not been in touch since the last twenty years. Wait, I think, it's been more than twenty years now," Rizwan confirmed casually and added, "It was just a casual fling, you know."

Vayu observed that Rizwan's hand was again scratching his stubble. Though he made a deadpan and cold face, his gestures revealed the storm in the core of his mind. He couldn't hide his desperate attempt to manifest his affair with Shanaya as an ignorable fact for the murder investigation from Vayu.

"Some relations don't fade even after twenty years, Mr Rizwan," Vayu remarked. Rizwan attempted to protest, but Vayu cut him short and asked, "What was the reason for your break-up?"

"See, it was mutual. Our relationship had lost the charm, and we decided to part ways. No hard feeling, grudges or argument," Rizwan replied with his usual ease, except his restless hand.

"And that casual fling which had stopped more than twenty years ago with a sweet ending note triggered you into a fistfight with your college friend. Strange! Isn't it?" Vayu had a lingering smile on his face while asking that question.

"That... that...fight was a different thing altogether. Out of the blue, Jignesh started insulting me. That had nothing to do with my equation with Shanaya," Rizwan fumbled, as if trying to buy some time to prepare his answer.

"But, according to the witnesses, Jignesh teased Shanaya in front of you about her relationship with you," Chaddha jumped in. He was determined not to allow any smallest possible chance for Rizwan to escape. It seemed, in his mind, he had already convicted Rizwan of murdering Shanaya.

Rizwan ran his fingers through his short hair and said, "I don't remember his exact wordings but his intention."

"Let me help you with what we have heard till now from the witnesses. You and Shanaya were having some discussion. Jignesh interfered, congratulating Shanaya for her successful business career and said that Shanaya must not be making any unwise decision as she used to do in her college life. Her experiences should have taught her the lesson that all shining things are not gold. She shouldn't allow any coward and opportunist people in her life who will turn their back on her when she needed them the most," Vayu narrated, reading Rizwan's face minutely and paused, expecting some response from him. Rizwan chuckled, resting his head back on his chair and looked up hopelessly.

"Jignesh hadn't even mention your name. Why did you take that as your insult? Do you consider yourself a coward and an opportunist?" Vayu asked.

"No! I don't. But I was aware of Jignesh's intention to insult me," Rizwan almost screamed as if he was trying hard to convince himself with his answer rather than Vayu and Chaddha.

An awkward silence usurped their conversation. Vayu and Chaddha exchanged a glance as they noticed Rizwan's moist eyes.

"I am not an opportunist. I was compelled to reject her marriage proposal back then," Rizwan broke the silence in a low and huskier voice. After a few more quiet moments, he said, "Being born in an orthodox Muslim family, I couldn't convince my parents to accept a Hindu daughter-in-law. Walking away from them holding Shanaya's hand wasn't an option either as I was just a college student then, completely dependent on my parents, having no source of income. It would have been suicide for both of us."

Rizwan continued, "She was in some deep shit. She had never told me as she didn't want me to marry her out of sympathy."

After a moment of silence, Vayu suggested, "You can leave. Take good rest, Mr Rizwan."

It was not the first time for him. Violence, the smell of blood, flesh, burnt skin, gun powder, disrupted human organs and distorted corpses couldn't even make him blink or frown. He had signed up for it when he became a cop. However, he had never planned and killed someone to satiate his vengeance. Killing a human whom he had kissed a moment before strangling her brutally. Killing a human outside of his duty and not even with an excuse of self-defence.

The lingering influence of the drug invited a brutal headache, drowsiness and nuisance while he tried hard to bandage his bleeding forearm. Somehow, he managed to wrap the wound after applying medicine and covering it with cotton, but his hand quivered severely. He rubbed his eyes to wipe away the blurriness of his vision, took a deep breath and tried to cut the bandage with a blade. But the sight of Oorja's bulging eyes, quaking tongue and helpless grope flashed before his eyes. He felt her warm breathing on his face. He pushed himself, swinging the blade through that bandage-cloth.

"Uff!" He groaned as the blade slit his forearm outside the wrapping. He limped towards the bathroom, turned on the basin tap and held that fresh wound underwater. It wasn't deep enough comparing to those scratches that Oorja had clawed.

"Fuck!" He screamed in irritation as his bandage and the cotton beneath got drenched. He had to unwrap the whole thing and start over. He saw something strange in the mirror out of the corner of his eyes. He hadn't noticed the mirror till then. He lifted his face and stared straight into the dark and deep eyes of that grinning man in the mirror. He resembled Abhimanyu but had a diabolic, distorted face covered in blood. Abhimanyu touched his face in disbelief to confirm that he was not smiling.

"Who are you?" Abhimanyu wasn't certain whether his voice was audible to the outside world or just inside his mind. However, his curiosity had been conveyed to that man inside the mirror, and he started laughing loudly.

"Fuck you!" Abhimanyu shouted with moist eyes and punched the mirror. The broken pieces of the mirror pierced his fist, letting the blood to spread out and scatter all over the basin and floor.

"Shit! Shit!" He shouted in pain.

He used his other hand to fetch his mobile out of his pocket as it rang, tucked it between his shoulder and tilted his head under the ear after receiving the call, and shouted, "Hello."

"Sir, DGP has arrived at the station and wants to meet you," a policeman responded.

"Hmm..."

"Do you want me to send someone to pick you up from your home?"

"Hmm...Yes."

"Please, let us know what you know about Shanaya and her murder, ma'am," Vayu asked as that lady in blue saree settled herself on the chair in front of them. She was fair, short and quite fat with a round face and long, black and neatly-braided hair. Her sharp nose looked awkward compared to the rest of her blunt and roundish features. Her short neck was overloaded with numerous golden chains competing with the number of bangles in her hands.

"I knew this long back...." She started stretching her big eyes wider.

But Chaddha interrupted her asking her name and occupation after catching a surprising glimpse of Vayu.

"Supriya Sinha, housewife," Vayu answered, lazily inclining his back a little more on the sofa and requested, "Please go ahead ma'am."

Supriya cleared her throat, adjusted herself oh her chair and started, "Okay! Let's start from the beginning then."

Vayu couldn't control his smile at the gossip lady. He knew what was coming.

"Though many of our college friends have been invited to Shanaya's birthday party, we four were quite close, like a gang. We used to go together everywhere, whether it was a movie, concert, disco, restaurant or bunking classes and hanging around in the campus," she continued with versatile dramatic expressions.

"You four means Shanaya, Supriya, Rizwan and Sachidananda, right?" Vayu asked to confirm his hunch with that static smile on his face.

Supriya nodded, affirming and advised them, "Don't call him Sachidananda; he doesn't..."

"You can skip that part," Chaddha interrupted frowningly. He seemed quite irritated with Supriya's freedom of speech as Vayu didn't ask her any specific, rather serious question, but she started blabbering her college story out of context.

"What about Jignesh? Wasn't he a part of your gang?" Vayu enquired.

Supriya inclined towards Vayu and whispered, oscillating her face along with her long earrings, "No way! He was a creepy guy who always used to find some or other meaningless excuses to talk with Shanaya. A total pervert. He used to beg, borrow, and sometimes steal money from other students as well. He was friendless, a loner in college. Rizwan warned and insulted him several times whenever he tried to socialize with us."

"How could you label someone who was just eager to talk as a pervert?" Chaddha snapped back as he didn't like her judgmental characteristic.

"Initially, Shanaya also thought the same, and she even had a heated argument with Rizwan as she admonished him to stop bullying Jignesh. But Jignesh misinterpreted Shanaya's intentions as her romantic inclination for him, and after a few days, he passed a letter to her. It was an indecent love letter. I don't remember clearly," Supriya continued along with her various modulations of tone and proper facial expression like an adept storyteller and paused momentarily, saying, "Hmm...wait, let me think."

"It's okay, ma'am. We can skip the detail of that letter as of now," Vayu suggested smiling and asked, "How did Shanaya and Rizwan react to that?"

"Shanaya slapped Jignesh after reading it, crumpled the paper, threw it on his face in front of our whole class and stormed out of the room without a single word," Supriya told under a single breath and started laughing.

Vayu laughed in unison, thinking to himself that people like Supriya can't be anyone's friend or enemy; they just enjoy the chaos, scandals, quandary, compulsion and misery of their lives. However, she was Vayu's joker in the pack, might turn into a magical key to unlock that mystery. "And Rizwan?" Vayu asked spontaneously.

"He went a few steps further and took full advantage of the situation. He forced Jignesh to strip, standing on the high bench, completely naked. Few other guys joined Rizwan to make that a grand entertainment and asked him to read that letter out loud, replacing Shanaya's name with his mother's name. Jignesh refused, but he had nothing in his control then.

The Sinful Silence • 51

They blackmailed him about taking that letter to the principal," Supriya said.

"That must be devastating for Jignesh! Isn't it? I mean, how did he gather himself together after that humiliation?" Vayu asked, pondering.

"He didn't come to college after that; only appeared in the exams. That was our final year. So, I haven't met him after that until yesterday at the party."

Vayu speculated whether that embarrassment in front of his classmates evolved into a potential stressor for Jignesh. Though he had mentioned that Shanaya had never misbehaved or insulted him, but that seemed like a partial truth to Vayu after listening to Supriya. Shanaya played a major part in that harassment.

"And why did they break up? I mean Rizwan and Shanaya," Vayu asked after prolonged humming.

"Okay, then what happened, you know, gradually Rizwan and Shanaya started meeting separately, avoiding the rest of us with an excuse of working on a business model," she told, expressing mirth.

She inched closer to Vayu and almost murmured, "They might fool others but not me. I knew it from the beginning that they were dating. Whenever we asked Rizwan or Shanaya to show us their project, they made some random excuses."

"Huh! You are a witty lady; we can see that from your appearance itself. We are literally counting on you to solve this murder," Vayu appreciated her, grinning.

Chaddha stared at Vayu, followed by a long sigh, and asked frustratingly, "Then?"

"Then god knows what happened; Shanaya just absconded. A few of our friends saw her last in an empty classroom, crying. She didn't even appear in the final exam." After a thoughtful pause, she continued, "That cheerful, naughty and hyperactive Rizwan had transformed into a living dead person after she left;

tranquil like a lifeless object. I tried my best to console him, but he was so obsessed with Shanaya that he convinced me to meet her and let him know her whereabouts."

"Did you meet her?" Vayu asked curiously, sensing an unexplored area.

"Yes, I went to her home almost after more than a year on Rizwan's repetitive insistence. He just couldn't get over her. I couldn't see him dying every day. He just gave up living," Supriya said slowly and softly, inattentive to her words, as if trying to visualize something.

Vayu noticed a glitter in her eyes; must be tears, he thought.

"I was predetermined to portray Shanaya as the worst person possible to Rizwan, irrespective of the consequence of my meeting with her; it would have helped him move on and lead a normal life," she murmured.

Vayu had to bend slightly forward to hear her clearly. Few drops of tears conglomerated at the corner of her eyes.

"But I didn't need to tell any lies to Rizwan. In reality, Shanaya was a bitch, more than I had planned to describe her," she told firmly in a louder tone. A tear rolled down her face. "She was pregnant. She had been trying hard to hide her baby bump with a pillow while talking to me, pretending that everything was normal. However, neither she mentioned anything about her pregnancy, nor I had any interest in asking."

Vayu accepted his misjudgement for Supriya. He corrected himself internally – She doesn't care about anyone, but him. He wondered whether that care for Rizwan made her another potential suspect. "Uff!" Vayu sighed in discomfort.

"It must not be Rizwan, I believe," Vayu remarked thoughtfully.

Supriya chuckled to say, "As I said, they didn't even have any mode of communication after she left college."

The Sinful Silence • 53

"Any idea, whose child it could be?" Chaddha enquired. She shook her head.

They were silent a few moments before Vayu enquired reluctantly, "I forgot to ask Rizwan… Do you know whether he is married or not?"

"Yes, he married a girl of his parents' choice."

"Thank you, ma'am!"

Supriya left the chair and approached the exit.

"Why didn't you speak your heart out to him?" Vayu asked as he stood up, leaving the couch.

She turned to him and told softly, "I don't know how to love a man who is emotionally dead."

Abhimanyu wasn't surprised to see his subordinates' serious faces, pretending to be busy in their allotted work when he reached the police station.

"DGP is waiting for you in your cabin," one of them informed him, wearing a concerned face.

Abhimanyu waggled towards his cabin, figuring out the best possible justification to defend himself. He speculated what could be the reason of his arrival to his station at almost 1.15 p.m.

"It must be because of that fucking reporter," he whispered, slapping himself to gather his scattered consciousness.

He tried hard to look sober as he tucked his white shirt inside his jeans, unfolded his sleeves, and buttoned the cuffs. That was the first time he was nervous about entering his fortress, his cabin.

"May I come in, sir?" he asked, pushing open the door partly.

"Yes, of course," DGP, Omprakash Bakshi responded loudly, gesturing Abhimanyu to come inside. Omprakash was in his late fifties, having a couple of years left for his retirement, and he wanted to spend that time peacefully.

He looked quite irritated as he frowned his wrinkled face and asked Abhimanyu to take a seat.

"Today is my daughter's birthday, and I had to leave my family function to meet you," Omprakash said at the top of his voice immediately after Abhimanyu parked himself on a chair. "After all, you are a celebrity now," he added, taking off his thick spectacles and placing them on the table.

"Your martial arts have become viral now. All the news channels have been playing it on loop, and they aren't getting tired of praising you. So proud of you, man!" Omprakash continued as Abhimanyu sat there tongue-tied.

Omprakash played one of the newsfeeds of Abhimanyu's scuffles with the reporters on his mobile and placed it on the table in front of him. Abhimanyu caught a glimpse of the screen reluctantly. The incident was titled 'Police *bane* Rambo' flashing at the bottom of the screen, and the news presenter had been screaming to portray Abhimanyu as an officer of the East India Company, brutalizing a freedom fighter.

Abhimanyu chuckled, complaining, "You know them, right sir? They just want something to raise the TRP."

"That's all you have in your defence? Not enough. Hundreds of cameras recorded this 'something' shit, and it has gone out of my control now. This 'something' might jeopardize your career, Abhi. Why can't you just ignore them and do your duty?" Omprakash shrieked as he abandoned the chair and started walking aimlessly in anger.

"I am sorry, sir. I was sleep-deprived and quite restless due to a few critical cases I am handling…I just lost my cool," Abhimanyu murmured, closing the news on the mobile.

"You didn't lose your cool; you have lost your mind permanently. A DCP is supposed to take care of a whole division, but you can't even handle a single police station. Demote yourself or resign if you think you are not capable. You have already proved your incapability on the past few occasions and compelled me to appoint Vayu as your backup," Omprakash snapped back, banging the table with his fist. A silence overpowered the cabin momentarily.

Omprakash went back to his chair and continued in a low voice, "You set a terribly wrong example for a rookie IPS officer on his very first day of duty; you killed four unarmed humans that night."

"Sir, we had no prior information about their numbers or weapons. And they attacked us as soon as we entered that house. You can see my fractured head," Abhimanyu pointed at his bandaged head and continued, "It was just self-defence, sir."

Omprakash started laughing and advised, "Keep all these stories for your defence in the court, Abhi. Vayu has already reported the incident in detail."

"*Madarchod*," Abhimanyu muttered.

"What?"

Abhimanyu shook his head to say, 'nothing.'

"Abhi, you are suspended for three months. I can't back you this time. I am getting tremendous pressure from my superiors, and they are not ready to listen to anything," Omprakash informed in a low voice.

Omprakash rose and reached closer to Abhimanyu at the other side of the table.

"Look at you! What you have done to yourself? There was a time you used to be the brightest officer in our department. Whatever happened was extremely unfortunate and awful, I agree. But you must move on, my boy! You can't change the past, but you can start afresh from where you are and make a better future," Omprakash advised, patting his back before leaving the cabin.

Abhimanyu leaned on the table and hid his face in his crossed arms.

"By the way, do you know someone called Mohammad Samim Chaudhary, a famous and influential name in the news media?" Omprakash enquired, returning to the cabin.

Abhimanyu turned back, shook his head, and lied, "No."

"He is taking your incident quite personally, spreading about it all over India and demanding for your termination from the police force. Anyway, take care Abhi!"

Omprakash left, leaving Abhimanyu pondering.

"**Arrey**, sir!" Chaddha shouted in excitement to see Vayu in the police station early in the morning.

Vayu didn't respond as two large headphone speakers covered his ears. He lounged in his chair, closing his eyes, either engrossed in listening to something or sleeping.

"Vayu sir!" Chaddha called again from his desk, busy arranging his tall metal lunch box and bag on the table. Not getting any response, he walked down to Vayu and pushed his shoulder softly. "Sir."

"*Yar*? ('who' in Tamil)," Vayu shrieked, startling.

"So...sorry to disturb you, sir," Chaddha fumbled nervously.

Vayu smiled, taking his headphones off, and told, "It's okay; I didn't notice you."

"Sir, you have broken my record today. I used to be the first person to reach office every day. This Dubey and everyone else make fun of me, saying that I should start sweeping and dusting the office before their arrival. So that the department doesn't need to pay the housekeepers anymore," Chaddha told grinning. He pulled a chair for himself, and sat on it.

"I couldn't sleep last night. I just kept on listening to the recording of our interrogation yesterday. Though still, we must dig a lot more on Rizwan, Jignesh, Sandy and Supriya. All of them seems like potential suspect to me. The sweet revenge story of Jignesh, the desperate chase of Sandy for his dream, the breakup of a steady and serious relationship between Rizwan and Shanaya just before Shanaya's pregnancy and the wounded heart of Supriya – anything could be the stressor to result in Shanaya's murder," Vayu said, brooding in the memory of yesterday's interrogation.

"Few characters are still left to be introduced into this story," Chaddha reminded, laughing.

"Yes, Shanaya's family, right? It's quite a lengthy suspect pool. But, before that, push all these four people under our surveillance 24/7," Vayu ordered.

"Yes sir, I will ask Dubey to arrange for it."

After spending some pondering moments, Vayu said softly, "The internet has lured us with easy access to anything and anyone. It has provided the curtains to hide people's real faces, taught us to fake our emotions and grant us the freedom of doing anything while staying anonymous. But it has also trapped our life and existence into little boxes."

Chaddha stared at Vayu for some moment and fumbled, "Cha…Chai?"

"No! I need their call histories of last twelve months and a hacker who can take us through all devices Shanaya owns," Vayu instructed. Chaddha nodded a yes.

"Let's go!" Vayu hopped out of his chair and rushed towards the exit.

"But where are we going?" Chaddha asked in shock, somehow managing to raise himself and his bulging belly from the chair.

"To meet Shanaya's family," Vayu answered loudly from a distance at the corridor, outside the station.

"Sir, but wouldn't 6 a.m. be too early for visiting someone?"

Chaddha didn't get any response as Vayu couldn't hear him from the parking.

Abhimanyu groped on the bed, looking for his mobile as its loud ringtone busted his sleep, but his hands didn't touch it. His eyelids were heavy; they weighed down as he tried to lift them. He had to put an effort to raise his eyelids halfway to fall down as his eyes were burning in the heat. He took a glimpse of the bed and found his mobile, glowing noisily on the bed, a little far from his reach.

"Uff!" He moaned in pain as he stretched his hand to grab the mobile. All the joints of his limbs and torso announced their existence with pains. He felt a furious headache and a layer of dehydrated, thick, salty saliva that coated his cracked lips. Somehow, he managed to voice the word, "Hello!" after receiving the call, ignoring the feel of pricking needles inside his throat.

"What happened, sir? Were you trying to reach me?" Chakra asked.

"Yes, I called you several times last night, but you didn't pick." Abhimanyu murmured in a drowsy voice.

"Sorry, sir. I had to keep my mobile back at home. *Aap ko to sab pata hai, apne dhande ka...* I was in a secret place, making a big deal of glowing tablets; people call it ecstasy. It's quite difficult to prepare requires a lab and some trained cooks."

"Do whatever you want, but don't sell your shit to any students," Abhimanyu admonished in a low voice.

"It will be an expensive crap for a student to afford. So, schools and colleges are not our targeted markets. But I can't take guarantee of those rich and spoilt brats who gather in those rave parties which are our prime trading locations."

Abhimanyu could only make a humming sound as his throat felt like sandpaper. He grabbed the water bottle from the bedside table, opened the cap in a hurry, and started gulping the water.

"The first few samples will go to you; it's a gift from my side. Just inform me if there is any plan for a raid," Chakra told, followed by a short laugh.

Abhimanyu gulped down the whole bottle and said, "I don't want to be the rat of your fucking lab." After a few mute moments, he continued, "I must be alive for a few more days till I complete my job… Anyway, the main reason I was trying to reach you is because I need the whereabouts of two men – Yusuf Malik and Suraj Kumar. They must be hiding somewhere in Faridabad. I will send you their pictures as soon as I get them."

"I will try my best, sir," Chakra assured.

"Okay, bye!" Abhimanyu dragged himself out of bed.

"Sir, I heard Harishchandra suspended you," Chakra checked.

"Harishchandra? You mean DGP Omprakash?" Abhimanyu said with a soft laugh and continued, "That guy is like a lotus in the muddy, murky water. Honest and simple, who has no clue of anything around him." After a pause, he asked, "How do you know about my suspension?"

"Kya sahib? Apna dhanda tips pe chalta hai. Otherwise, it's impossible to avoid raids, and that's why you remembered me to find these two men. *Hai na apna panter log, aap ke* department *mein."*

"Who are they?" Abhimanyu enquired quickly.

"Rahene do na Sahib, leave it."

Abhimanyu disconnected the call.

Shanaya's residence at the outskirts of Noida, sector 150, was quite far from their police station at sector 18; it was a drive of almost fifty minutes in normal traffic. A cool breeze brushed Vayu's face as he lowered the window-glass of their SUV. A smile waved on his upper lip, covered under his neatly kempt moustache, thinking that there couldn't be a better start for him than Shanaya's murder case. The pressure was tremendous which had been mounting with each passing hour.

"In the middle of difficulty lies opportunity," Vayu whispered, looking at the horizon.

"*Hanji?*" Chaddha asked in surprise, taking a quick glance at Vayu by his driving seat before laying his eyes back on the road.

"Nothing, Einstein's quote."

"Sir, what was the point of asking their names, occupations and relationships with Shanaya while we had been aware of all those from the sheet that the manager had provided." Chaddha was curious, keeping his eyes glued on the street. He glimpsed at Vayu, turned his face back on the road, and continued laughing, "I know, it's a stupid question, but I have been thinking about this since last night. I had thought of asking you at the end yesterday itself, but completely forgot in the hurry of returning home.

"First stop calling me sir; it's weird from a man of my father's age," Vayu demanded with a smile. Chaddha nodded a 'yes,' stealing a glance at Vayu in between his driving.

"Of course, we know the answers to those petty questions, and that's why they are important to set up the base of reactions, facial expressions, and body language of a suspect. This is exactly how a lie detector works," Vayu started explaining.

"So, do you mean, reactions, facial expressions and body language change when someone lies?" Chaddha asked with a bright smile, expecting a 'yes' from Vayu.

Vayu nodded and said, "Human eyes, lips, forehead, nose, hand, legs and even vocal tone and choice of words change with emotion. They are our recording parameters in the absence of a polygraph machine."

Chaddha grinned in amusement.

"Humans can be trained to fake all these superficial and physical signs of lying with proper training, but that's impossible for common people." Vayu muted for a moment and thoughtfully said, "Unfortunately, all of Shanaya's four friends either lied or hid some truths."

"Ahh!" Abhimanyu inhaled the steam from his coffee mug. He sipped a few drops of it. The first milky sip crept over his tastebuds and rolled down his throat like a pair of soft lips brushing him from inside. He was not so fond of coffee before Ahi had stepped into his life. Unconsciously, he had started adopting Ahi's habits, dialects, behaviours, even her complete existence while loving her. Ahi's favourite black coffee without milk and sugar was beyond unpleasant bitterness for him. He tapped the coffee's murky surface to break the thickening layer, pondering in Ahi's memory. The warm brown drink dripped from his finger, the ripples spreading towards the rim in ever-larger circles inside the mug. "Ahi!" he murmured, remembering how she used to wrap her fingers around her coffee-mug like a delicate flower, savouring the warmth that spread through her soft and pink palms.

The caffeine helped him break the cloud of drugs in his mind and the busted slothfulness in his blood flow. He felt much more comfortable and in control.

Abhimanyu picked up his mobile as Dubey's number popped up on the screen and said, "What's up, Dubey ji."

"Sir, we are at a lodge named 'Drive inn' by Greater Noida Expressway. The staff here found a female victim strangled to death. The name of the victim is Oorja Shah, twenty-eight years old according to her voter card," Dubey reported under one breath.

"Any eyewitnesses?" Abhimanyu could hear his thumping heart beneath his ribcage.

"No, sir. Could you please come here and have a look at the scene? I couldn't get hold of Vayu and Chaddha; they are busy with Shanaya Mehta's case."

Abhimanyu sighed a breath of relief. "Actually, I am s..." he checked his word and muted for a moment. A morbid curiosity got the best him to say, "I am coming."

Chaddha turned his metallic chariot and slid through a muddy path at the left towards the highway. Both of them stared at the GPS screen in disbelief as they didn't believe their rich homicide victim had been residing there. Chaddha reluctantly shifted the gear to one, compelled to drive on that bumpy, slippery, curvy and muddy path. After a few sharp turns, they reached in front of a huge mansion, surrounded by lush green lawns and neatly maintained gardens.

"I believe we have reached," Vayu murmured in amusement, gluing his eyes on the palace in front of them.

The mansion loomed proudly from behind the iron gate, hinged with two squared-shaped pillars on either side. A wooden nameplate was fastened on the pillar at the right side. It read – 'Mehta's nest'.

"What's her husband's name?" Vayu asked, reading the nameplate.

"Manoj Sharma," Chaddha answered, looking at the rear windshield as he drove the vehicle in reverse gear to park it properly.

"Interesting, especially in an Indian patriarchy society." Vayu murmured to himself.

That two-storied mansion was widely spread at the edge of a village, in the middle of agricultural lands by the Greater Noida Expressway. It was designed to give it the appearance of a huge hut in the centre of a large garden. They heard the birds chirping, sounds of flowing water and rustling leaves as Chaddha shut down the ignition of his SUV.

"It's there," Vayu pointed out the switch of the doorbell just below the nameplate. Chaddha was still looking for it.

A young man opened the iron gate, making a loud clang of metal, even before Chaddha had rung the doorbell. He must be the security guard, not expecting a visitor so early in the morning. He had hurriedly wrapped himself in a blue unbuttoned shirt of his uniform on top of printed shorts. His eyes were puffy and bloodshot, and the hair was messy like a nest. Vayu introduced himself and Chaddha, flashing his ID. The man asked them to follow him and guided them to a giant living room inside the mansion.

"Please wait here," he requested, pointing at the three couches placed in a circle around a wooden centre table at the middle of the hall. Then, he disappeared somewhere inside the building.

Chaddha lounged against the soft backrest of one of the couches covered in dark green silky fabric, spreading his arms wide – one on the ornate wooden armrest and another on the backrest.

"Vayu," Chaddha had a thrill in his voice as he pawed the couch.

The wooden floor was covered with a furry carpet. The walls around were overloaded with family pictures and a few large portraits of Shanaya with a man who could be perfectly referred as beautiful rather than handsome, and a few with a girl who was a carbon copy of younger Shanaya. There was another full-body portrait of that beautiful man, posing with a guitar in a white leather jacket and trousers. His hair was neatly back-brushed, leaving two long sideburns, which widened as it progressed towards the jaw lines. He had a sharp nose just above his clean-shaved philtrum and chin. His lips were thin and red, like he had applied lipstick before the photo session. Vayu smiled as that portrait reminded him of Elvis Presley. Vayu had been staring at those photos since he stepped inside the mansion; he couldn't hear Chaddha's voice.

"A picture speaks a thousand words... sometimes the entire story of a life," Vayu whispered to himself as a smile lingered his lips.

There was a bamboo tree, fenced at the corner. Vayu walked close to that tree and touched it.

"It's real," a male voice, pleasing to the ears, said at his back.

Vayu turned around to find a tall, fair, middle-aged man in white kurta and pyjama. He looked like a wreckage of that attractive man in those portraits – baldpate, dark circles under his eyes, double chin, hanging fleshy cheeks and a bulged tummy in a lean torso.

"I am not sure whether 'good morning' will be the proper greeting in the current scenario, Mr Manoj Sharma," Vayu said, returning to the couches.

"Please have a seat," Manoj requested Vayu.

"Why did you..." Vayu checked his words, leaving his question unfinished and gestured at Chaddha to lead the interrogation.

Some curiosities that knocked Vayu's mind while looking through those portraits made him impatient enough to commit that same mistake which he did with Supriya. Jumping to a conclusion based on circumstances. He didn't want to repeat his mistake.

"Did... did you notice anything weird in Shanaya's behaviour lately?" Chaddha fumbled to buy some time to frame his question. Manoj shook his head negative no, almost spontaneously.

"What do you do for a living, Mr Sharma?" Vayu interfered.

Manoj answered after a few seconds of silence, "I am a stock investor."

"I see!" There was a glee of small success in Vayu's voice as he had guessed the unsteady financial condition of Shanaya's husband from the nameplate outside the gate. "It must be a rollercoaster ride, right? I mean, sometimes big wins and sometimes bigger losses; quite unsteady, isn't it?"

"Tell me about it!" Manoj said softly.

In the meanwhile, a woman arrived with a large tray. She placed the tray on the table in front of them, obeying the gesture from Manoj and offloaded the tray, placing three cups of tea and a plate of biscuits on the table.

"Do you have any group to invest together, or you do it individually? I mean, how do you do the disaster recovery?" Vayu enquired, lifting a cup of tea from the table.

"Officer, I don't know how these questions are relevant to Shanaya's murder. I am in a devastating state of mind right now. So, please spare me from this nonsense," Manoj pleaded, holding his palms together.

Chaddha picked his cup of tea following Vayu and solaced, "We can understand what you are going through, but it's our duty. We have to analyse every aspect."

"Aspect? Do you mean I killed her for money as I have lost all my money in the stock market? Bullshit! I manage my own money," Manoj pitched his voice quite high in a wave of anger.

"We didn't mean anything, Mr Sharma. Your agitation indicates that you are not doing good financially. In fact, you are in a financial crunch despite having a rich spouse," Vayu stated firmly. Not getting a reply from Manoj, Vayu continued, "In seventy percent of the homicide cases in India, the spouses were found guilty. I am afraid all these circumstances and statistical facts shouldn't misguide us."

"Yes, my financial condition is not good," Manoj shrieked, and after few mute moments, he started in a low voice. "I had to take loans from some local usurers to close a few of my previous loans from banks. I didn't realize that I have been worshiping a demon to get rid of some wild dogs. Banks would have been much better than these goons who can go to any extent to snatch their money back. Excessive interest, insults, mental and physical abuses and death threats are an integral part of my life now."

"Why didn't you ask your wife for help?" Chaddha asked.

"She did help me several times before, but not this time." Manoj's voice gradually dropped into silence.

"So, you had no option other than kill your wife to settle the score with those goons?" Vayu commented, dipping a biscuit into his tea.

"No, believe me!" Manoj shouted. "I...I am telling you everything clearly, just to buy your trust. I am still in debt; you can cross-check my bank statement."

"Okay, I trust you as of now," Vayu murmured while his whole concentration was to rescue the biscuit, which had sunk into his tea. He smiled on his success in saving the biscuit and asked, "So, how are your child or children coping with this unfortunate scenario?"

Manoj chuckled softly, replying, "We don't have a child.

Vayu and Chaddha exchanged a squint as the reminiscences of Supriya's words made them uncomfortable.

"Being childless even after twenty years of conjugal life... was there any miscarriage or complication in delivery or any deficiency from either of you? I know it's a private matter and quite insensitive to ask, but we are bound by our duties." Vayu seemed quite disturbed while enquiring as he sniffed something suspicious, which botched his mind's tranquillity.

Manoj chuckled softly, replying, "Neither of them. We didn't even try for a kid because Shanaya didn't want it. And it's fifteen years since we have been married, not twenty." He leaned on the centre table, picked up his cup of tea and continued after adjusting back his posture on the couch. "Poonam was quite young when we got married; completely dependent on Shanaya after her parents' demise. So, Shanaya decided not to have our own kid because managing her father's business as a novice and raising up Poonam with proper care had absorbed all her time and energy."

Manoj added, reading their muddled faces, "Oh, Poonam is my sister-in-law, Shanaya's sister," and pointed at that portrait in which Shanaya was pouting with a lookalike girl.

They turned their faces to the wall while Manoj continued, "Actually, she is the daughter from Shanaya's mother's second marriage, stepsister. But they are one soul in two bodies. She doesn't stay with us anymore as the grown-up girl desires for some personal space."

"That's a lot," Vayu murmured, turned his face back to Manoj. "Didn't you marry Shanaya during her final year in college?"

"No! As I said, when I met Shanaya for the first time in a bar, she had already taken over her stepfather's business due to his sickness. And he died after a couple of years of our marriage," Manoj confirmed.

"I see." Vayu smiled thinking of the institution called marriage. It is called an institution because we learn the lessons of life here – we learn to let go of our ego for the sake of relationships and love, we learn to stay together, no matter what. We learn to stick with each other through our ups and downs, ignore the flaws, and embrace the positive qualities. However, sometimes this institution misguides us to overlook our childhood's basic learning – we shouldn't trust a stranger blindly. Vayu wondered how Shanaya and Manoj had spent fifteen years of their lives together under the same roof, incognizant of each other like two strangers.

"So, having no child is the reason you have given up on your life?" Vayu tried to dig deeper.

"What do you mean?" Manoj asked, frowning after a pause of sipping his tea.

"I mean, look at your pictures! How an aspiring Elvis Presley has turned into an older man before his time? Do you still sing or practise at least?"

Manoj laughed softly, staring at the largest portrait of Shanaya and told in delay. "That was my young, illusory mind, filled with the dreams of touching the sky. But life eventually teaches us to walk on the brutal ground of reality. It's just age that changes your perception, appearance and even your entire existence."

Silence drenched the ambience in a suffocating awkwardness.

Vayu thought, 'Why the hell is Manoj staring at Shanaya's portrait while talking about his apathy towards his own life? Shouldn't he look at his own pictures to decide whether my question is justified or not? He is definitely hiding something.'

"Or maybe Shanaya is the reason? What is it, Mr Sharma?" Vayu asked on an impulse.

Manoj was mute for a few moments and said, "Nothing like that."

"Thanks for your time, Mr Sharma! Your contribution will greatly help our investigation." Vayu raised himself from the couch.

"Can you get us all her electronic devices and Poonam's address?" Chaddha asked. Vayu made an appreciative gesture as he had forgotten about that completely.

Manoj nodded and departed. After a few minutes, that woman who had served them tea arrived and handed over a bag-pack to Chaddha, which had two mobile phones, two laptops and one tablet.

"*Yeh bhi.*" She forwarded a visiting card and a piece of paper with Poonam's address to Vayu.

Vayu looked at the card and whispered after reading, "Psychologist? Interesting!"

Abhimanyu found it difficult to ride his Royal Enfield up to the crime scene at Drive Inn. The majestic faintness and floating effects of the drugs, which always cocooned him from all the pain and chaos of his mind, left a nasty tipsiness, headache and nausea. The sun was up when he started, evaporating the chillness of early morning and drenching his shirt in sweat. He spat a couple of times to get rid of that intolerably bad taste in his mouth. His hands shivered while manoeuvring his metallic horse. The thumping sounds of its engine, which he used to love like a soothing romantic song, had been hammering his head. He had to stop his bike at the edge of the highway before dashing any other vehicle or toppling over the road. He got off the bike, resting it on the side stand and fetched a small pouch from his pocket. His hand trembled severely as he put his index finger inside that pouch to pull out a tablet. He was aware that the venomous snakes he had been pampering in his veins and blood wouldn't sleep without swallowing that toxic tablet. He placed the tablet on his tongue and gulped it. He drew a water bottle from that small bucket attached to his bike, and swigged down water. He started for his destination as he gathered his strength after a few minutes.

"Jai Hind, sir," a policeman greeted Abhimanyu on the way to enter the motel. He felt dizzy and empty-headed while he nodded to acknowledge him. He found nobody at the reception, exactly how it was in his last visit as he walked inside. All the lights at the reception area and the corridor through which he headed to Oorja's room were on. 'Why the hell do these people have all the lights on? Isn't it morning now?' He thought and felt weird witnessing the darkness outside the motel through a window at the reception area. He reached Oorja's room, dragging his trembling feet on the floor of that narrow corridor. The door was ajar, and he pushed it open and entered the room. There was no one except a bare-bodied man, wrapping something in a huge plastic sheet. He wondered where the hell was Dubey and other policemen? Who the fuck was that guy? He rubbed his eyes to identify the man and the object inside that polythene wrap. The man had a glimpse of his face with a smile as he lifted that wrap on his shoulder. Abhimanyu was startled to identify himself, carrying the naked woman's dead body in that wrap and entering the bathroom.

He heard a male voice at his back, quite sharp and close to his ears, asking, "Are you okay, sir?"

Everything started changing in front of his eyes in a blink, as if someone had chanted some magical incantations. He could see the bright daylight outside; a beam of sunrays fell on the floor through the only open window of that room. The room was crowded with policemen who were busy collecting all possible shreds of evidence. And there was Dubey, standing close to him, asking, "Sir, are you okay?"

Abhimanyu nodded a yes.

"The dead body has been dumped there," Dubey informed, proceeding towards the bathroom.

Abhimanyu entered the lavatory following Dubey to find Oorja's naked dead body kept in a sitting posture, resting her back on the wall under the running shower. Few vivid visions of Oorja's bulging eyeballs swelled up his throat, her trembling legs flapping on the floor, and her groping, swatting hands and scratching nails, flashed through his mind like a film running at high speed.

"Such a clever bastard!" Dubey said softly, staring at the cadaver. Abhimanyu looked at him blankly.

"All the pieces of evidence are washed-out, sir. No fingerprints, skin tissues, hair, saliva or semen, except that bruise around the throat and neck. Strangled with hands but must have used gloves; we haven't found any fingerprints," Dubey informed, disappointingly.

"Anything suspicious in the room…" Abhimanyu asked, hoping a negative response.

"It's strange, but we didn't find anything."

"Any witness who might have seen something unusual?" Abhimanyu was curious whether he had left any trace behind.

"There are three men who take care of this whole property. One of them sits at the reception, and the rest two take care of the maintenance, cleaning and room services. Except for that reception guy, no one stays here after evening, and he didn't notice anything. They have one CCTV camera just behind the reception desk, but that doesn't work."

Abhimanyu was quite relaxed while asking, "Any other guests?"

"There are ten rooms, and only one was occupied last night; this one," Dubey replied, handing over Oorja's voter card, and continued, "According to her voter card, she is from a village in Rajasthan."

Abhimanyu came out of that room along with Dubey and lit a cigarette. He inhaled a lungful of smoke and instructed, letting the smoke out through his nose and mouth, "Keep looking for some clues and contact the nearest police station to her village and get hold of her family."

"Yes, sir."

Abhimanyu ambled out of the motel and walked across to the parking area in front of it. He pulled out his mobile from the pocket and searched for the mobile number of Purshottam Sastri. But before he could make the call, an unknown number popped up on his mobile screen.

"Hello, who is this?" Abhimanyu asked.

"Good morning, Abhimanyu. This is Purshottam Sastri," the calm and composed voice responded.

There were twenty numbers that Abhimanyu had saved in his phone as Purshottam's contact. However, he never used the same number to contact him, except one which was publicly declared as his office number. He always used that for formal conversations. Lately, Abhimanyu had given up that effort of saving numbers.

"Morning sir, I was about to call you regarding a bad incident," Abhimanyu said, sucking at the cigarette butt.

"I know, and that's what I am calling you. Reach Ooraj's home right now, clean up all the stuff related to the syndicate and give me a missed call on my official number when you are done." There was no remorse or grief in his voice, insensitively serene as usual.

"I had a similar plan. Unfortunately, I... I am suspended for three months. You have to find someone else to clean this shit," Abhimanyu fumbled in anxiety.

"Let me take care of that. You just work on my instruction; that's crucial at this moment," Purshottam ordered softly.

Abhimanyu was flooded with relief and said, "Thank you, sir!" That was his only chance to get the pictures of Yusuf Malik and Suraj Kumar and to wipe out any other traces which could connect him to Oorja.

"By the way, what's the progress on Shanaya Mehta's case? The opposition is making a lot of noise. I had a meeting with the MP, and she is quite worried about that case. Election is approaching soon, and the whole nation is looking at that homicide. Moreover, she was one of the members of my business group," Purshottam sounded concerned.

"We are working hard on it, sir. If we get the post-mortem report quickly, we can draw a conclusion in a week or two," Abhimanyu said whatever came to his mind.

"Okay, I will expedite the process," Purshottam disconnected the call.

"Five years...approximately," Vayu muttered, gluing his eyes on the visiting card of that psychologist, Dr R.K. Khanna.

Chaddha threw a glance at Vayu and concentrated on his driving, turning his face back on the road. "Five years, sir?"

Vayu looked at Chaddha, taking his eyes away from that visiting card and explained, "We have no information about five years of Shanaya's life; between her abandoning college and her marriage, when she was pregnant."

He looked at the horizon and questioned, "Who was that man, if not Manoj or Rizwan? And where is that child?" He kept losing the tempo, and the magnitude of his voice, which fell into complete silence.

Chaddha frowned, disturbed at his inadequacy to catch that gap.

Vayu looked excited as he suggested, "Let's meet Mr R.K. Khanna first, then we will talk to Poonam. Her psychologist might know the answers about what we are looking for."

Chaddha rotated the steering-wheel swiftly.

Abhimanyu parked his bike on the main road and walked into a blind alley which led to Oorja's residence at sector 41. It was an independent, single storied house at the end of that narrow back street. The thundering sound of his bike must have invited some undesirable attention of the inhabitants of that quiet locality. He slipped his hand in the back pocket of his jeans and sneaked out a bunch of keys, the only thing he had stolen from Oorja's clutch after killing her. A low wall surrounded the house with a small iron gate in the front. He glanced over the area around the house; couldn't see anyone. He thought of crossing the wall leaping over instead of wasting time on finding the right key from that bunch for that huge, metal lock hanging from that gate. However, on second thought, he refrained from doing anything stupid in broad daylight. He tried a few keys based on their shapes and sizes.

A huge shadow of a human startled Abhimanyu, and his trembling hand failed to aim the keyhole. He turned back in haste to face a gigantic man in white vest and lungi with checks. Abhimanyu raised his eyebrow along with his face and gestured to ask what he wanted. That man kept staring at the lock, ignoring him. His attitude puzzled Abhimanyu; raced his heart. There was so much going on in his head. He wondered whether that man was just a curious passer-by or someone from the syndicate, who was assigned to keep an eye on her home.

"*Kya hai?*" Abhimanyu asked sullenly.

That man grabbed the bottom of his lungi, slightly lifting it, held both sides of it and wrapped it around his waist. However, neither did he answer Abhimanyu nor glanced at him for once. Abhimanyu was irritated to such an extent that he thought of taking out his gun, putting the barrel inside the butthole of that man and firing. After hanging around for a few more seconds, that man started walking away lethargically. Abhimanyu kept staring at him until he reached the main road and disappeared eventually.

Abhimanyu was well acquainted with the house as he had met Oorja there a couple of times. He crossed the hallway which opened into a garden at the backyard and entered the first room at the left. He combed every nook and corner of that room hurriedly and approached the other room. He didn't find anything relevant to the syndicate in that room; there was nothing except household stuff. He couldn't find anything in the second room as well, even after searching under the bed, table, chairs, every shelf of that only cupboard in the house and behind all the wall hangings, pictures and locks. He extended his search operation to the kitchen and bathroom, but all his efforts were in vain. He was exhausted and frustrated as he pulled a chair for himself and lounged on it in the middle of the hallway. The only place which was left out to search was the garden. But a garden shouldn't be a safe place to hide the documents, he thought. However, his self-justification couldn't solace him even for a few seconds. He abandoned the chair abruptly and rushed toward the garden. He entered the garden area.

A well-maintained lawn occupied most of the garden area, leaving a narrow muddy surface along the boundary wall. And different types and sizes of plants and trees were planted only on that area of bare soil. A small iron-table was placed in the middle of the lawns, accompanied by two iron chairs of the same kind. Abhimanyu walked across the garden several times, thoroughly scanning every inch of it, but failed to find anything.

Each of his vain attempts increased his anxiety as he would not get another chance to visit that place. Moreover, he was cognizant of the sharpness of Vayu's twisted brain. He couldn't afford to leave any trace, not the tiniest hint that could link him with Oorja. He started sweating, his legs quivered as he returned to the hall, empty-handed. He started knocking all over the wall insanely, hoping for some hollow portion that could hide a secret chamber or something. However, he didn't find anything there. He reopened the cupboard, took out all the clothes, threw them on the floor and started knocking its interior. A devilish smile lit his face as he found a small door inside the closet, which led him to a secret shelf in the wall at the back. He moved the closet a little away from the wall, making a narrow passage between the wall and the cupboard and entered that narrow space. There were lots of documents, contact details, pictures of both the members of the syndicate and its victims, and a gun. He picked up a jute-bag from the kitchen and bagged all of them in that. He took some time to arrange all things he had touched back into its place.

Chaddha turned the steering to enter the slanted concrete alley, which led them to the parking of a multi-storeyed, commercial building. He parked his four-wheeler, occupying the only empty space. They walked towards the lift lobby after getting off the vehicle as per the direction of a security guard.

"I can't digest the fact that Shanaya was crazy," Chaddha remarked, reaching the lift lobby. Vayu laughed, pressing the button of the elevator.

"Why are you laughing? None of their friends or husband mentioned about her craziness. Moreover, how can an insane person do business?" Chaddha looked puzzled.

They got into the lift as the door opened after a ding.

"Not all of what is considered mental illness would necessarily fit under the term 'madness'," Vayu said, noticing they had no company in the lift. Chaddha nodded, pouting to convey his incomprehension.

Vayu continued with a smile, "Madness doesn't exist, mental illness does. We call a person mad only when the mental illness of that person is incomprehensible, untreatable and dangerous. Mental illness is not any of those things. Not all mentally ill people behave weirdly in public. People who suffer from depression, anxiety or phobias behave like you and me. In fact, all of us are mentally ill to a certain extent."

"You mean slightly mad? *Halka sa matlab*," Chaddha remarked, which made Vayu burst out laughing. Chaddha joined him.

They came out of the elevator as it stopped on the sixth floor and approached the reception.

"We are here to meet Dr Khanna," Vayu informed the lady at the reception desk.

The lady couldn't recognize them as cops because both were dressed in civil attire and asked, "Do you have an appointment?"

Chaddha flashed his batch and ordered, "Quick, we don't have time for your appointment and all."

"Yes, sir!" The lady stood up from her chair. She looked nervous while rushing into the chamber, pushing the large glass-door by the reception desk.

Chaddha lounged on a sofa opposite to that glass-door. Vayu's eyes were glued on the large portrait of Buddha, fastened on the wall behind that couch. It was an oil painting of the golden half face of Buddha; a lengthy and half nose extended upwards to construct an arch of the eyebrow, just above the stretched and ajar eye, soaked in peace and sanctified in mediation. Just beneath the shadowy philtrum, there was a half-pair of tranquil lips. An illuminated, half orb around his ornamental head made the navy-blue background darker. The shadow and light played a magnificent game.

"Weird," Vayu whispered, gazing at that painting.

Chaddha stood up, witnessing discomfort on Vayu's face. He turned his face to that painting and said, "What's weird here? Because it's half? Arrey Vayu, it's modern art. *Adha, tedha-medha, kuchh bhi chalta hai.*"

Vayu glanced at Chaddha, smiled, pointed out that dark navy-blue portion of the canvas, and told softly, "Someone is there."

Chaddha leaned on that painting to take a closer look at it. He could see a dark and half face just behind that golden one, almost invisible to the eyes as that golden face had been absorbing all the attention and visibility. That was another Buddha's face with an open eye, a diabolic smile, and messed up long hair spread across the rest of the canvas.

"Hmm... modern art *hai, kuch bhi chalta hai*," Chaddha echoed after some thoughtful moment.

"Sir, please come in," the receptionist requested them to follow her inside, opening that glass-door partly.

She led them to a large room through a corridor. A tall, aged dapper man welcomed them with a pleasant smile and introduced himself as Dr Rahul Kumar Khanna. He had long brownish hair, casually partitioned at the left, letting the long locks drop at both sides of his pale face, covering the ears and partly his wrinkled forehead. His face had chiselled features, defined cheekbones a confident and brown pair of eyes, pointed nose, thin lips and sharp jaw lines. Age had gifted him with a few loose folds of skins on his throat, which he covered beneath his nicely kempt pepper-salt beard. His black, square-framed spectacles hid those few wrinkles under his eyes. He looked fit in his grey vest suit, on a sky-blue shirt and grey trousers of the same fabric. The phrase 'aging with grace' was made for people like him.

A refreshing and mild fragrance stroke Vayu's senses as he stepped into that room. It enticed Vayu for lengthening his breathing period, making his olfactory receptors craving for more of that smell. As a result of changing the breathing pattern, he started feeling more relaxed and calmer.

"Would you like to have tea or coffee?" Rahul asked, gesturing them to sit on a couch. He had a British dialect in his low, heavy and thunderous voice. The low rumble of his voice was comforting enough to convince anyone that he could change everything wrong in the world.

"Tea," Chaddha was quick to grab the offer. Vayu shook his head in the negative.

"Anita, please arrange some tea and snacks for my guests," Rahul ordered, wrapping his words in the flavour of a request.

One might find Rahul over-polite, or dramatically civilized. However, he was more like a poetic king in his secluded palace.

That large room, rather the hall, was distinctly separated into two fragments. The portion in front of the entrance had a large wooden table, accompanied by a few small wooden chairs of similar kind and one different chair with heightened, cushioned backrest and decorated hand-rest. The other portion was occupied by two wide and expensive couches, covered in exotic, red fabric, a centre table and a chair, more like a throne. The chair was carved of fine oak, crested with several jewels and decorative metals forming an elegant coat of arms and heightened but slanted backrest. Several tall bookshelves covered the walls, leaving few portions for a flat-screen TV, an antique wall clock and two large windows.

"How can I help you, gentlemen?" Rahul enquired, softly reclining on his throne.

"I am sure you already know about the death of Mrs Shanaya Mehta," Chaddha started the conversation, noticing Vayu still pondering.

"Yup! That's horrible news," Rahul said, sighing and added after remorseful silence, "And it's sad that police have no clue even after thirty-six hours. Moreover, your DCP is busy with his boxing practice, making some innocent reporters as his punch-bag. Sad! So sad!"

"That's why we are here, Dr Khanna. We need your help in knowing Shanaya a little deeper," Vayu interfered, staring at another large painting.

Chaddha followed Vayu's eyes to find the painting and chuckled, whispering, "Modern art."

The painting of Buddha at the reception area was much better than this one according to him. He wondered whether a kid had scribbled something meaningless on a large canvas. There was a half wall-clock at the right edge of the canvas; few small dolphins and eagles were scattered all over the canvas and there was a mess of overlapping geometrical shapes, which kept changing colour on those overlapping portions.

Vayu turned his face away from the painting, looked straight at Rahul's eyes and asked, "What was her exact reason to visit you?"

"Obviously for counselling, some stress issues, anger management and disorientation," he answered vaguely.

In the meanwhile, Anita returned with two cups of tea and some biscuits on a tray.

"So, what's the root cause? What might be the possible reason for her issues?" Vayu asked.

"Pressure, what else? The pressure of Shanaya's huge business, jobless husband, and raising her immature sister. She was really stressed." Rahul's magical voice convinced both Vayu and Chaddha.

"Ohh! We are not aware of the condition of her sister. We are yet to meet her," Vayu said as he stood up from the couch and walked down to the corner of the room, near a shelf.

"We didn't find any sign which could convince us about the presence of any other human or species at the crime scene. No weapon too. There was no blood, no injury on the victim's body, no semen, saliva or broken hair, no damaged or broken property," Vayu explained, carefully examining the things on the shelf and continued, "Moreover, she shut the door from inside and made a call to the reception to wake her up in the morning. No one entered that room until the next morning when the manager opened the door with a duplicate key."

Rahul laughed softly, mocking, "Oh shit! So you guys are just beating around the bush now? Oh god!"

Chaddha looked quite offended at the remark. However, Vayu seemed indifferent, absorbing the things on the shelf.

Vayu hummed opening that shelf and asked, "What are these CDs for?"

"They are the recordings of my client's sessions. It helps me in my research and study." Rahul basked pride in his job.

"So, what do you know about Shanaya's life through your sessions so far?" Vayu asked, fetching a black box which had a white label stuck on it – Shanaya Mehta, followed by a number.

"What everyone knows about her, nothing special which can... can help you in your investigation," Rahul fumbled to manage his words. "You are not supposed to touch them. Those CDs have confidential, private and sensitive information about my clients." He admonished, raising his voice as he abandoned his throne and rushed to Vayu.

Chaddha followed him, dropping his teacup in a hurry.

"Either you have to tell us everything that you know about her life or you have to hand over these CDs," Vayu retorted calmly, holding that pack of CDs firmly in his hand. He continued after a tiny thoughtful pause, "You know what, we don't want to know anything from you. We will find whatever we need from these CDs."

"You can't take them without a court order. I have a contract with my clients, and I must obey that; it's my professional ethics," Rahul roared like a lion. His voice echoed.

"Dr Rahul Kumar Khanna, we can arrest you right now for being an obstacle in a murder investigation. It's a highly escalated case; everyone at the top level is closely watching its progress. And we have been given special permission to do whatever necessary for solving this case without any delay," Vayu admonished under one breath.

Chaddha was surprised to hear about that special permission.

"The bottom line is that we don't need any court order for this particular case," Vayu concluded firmly as he started rushing towards the door with that pack of CDs. He didn't want to give

Rahul any chance to break any further conversation. Chaddha followed him. Rahul kept standing there like a statue, staring at their departure.

Immediately after getting into the elevator, Chaddha said, "Vayu, are you crazy? We don't have any such special orders. If he complains about us, we will be suspended for sure. We are dealing with some really influential people here."

"We can't wait for a court order, Chaddha ji. He might tamper these videos if he is the man we are looking for," Vayu replied, looking a little nervous. "How many days will it take to get a court order?" he asked.

"It depends," Chaddha answered disappointingly.

"Get one quickly!"

Chaddha nodded. After a thoughtful mute moment, he looked at Vayu with bulged eyes and shocked expression and voiced his concern, "We forgot to take the prescription."

"What prescription?" Vayu asked.

"Dr Khanna must have prescribed some medicines for Shanaya, right? We should have to cross-check them. I had worked on a case where the family physician of a victim had prescribed some illegal drugs and under the influence of those drugs, convinced the patient to nominate the doctor as the sole inheritor after victim's death," Chaddha explained his concern.

"Dr Khanna is a psychologist, not a psychiatrist," Vayu said. "Both psychiatrists and psychologists understand how the human brain works, our emotions, feelings and thoughts. Both can treat mental illness with psychological treatments, which means conversation therapy. But psychiatrists attend medical colleges before they specialize in mental health, and they are authorized to prescribe medicine. Psychologists can't prescribe medicine as they are not doctors."

"Then why does Khanna write 'Dr' in front of his name?" Chaddha asked.

"He must have done a Ph.D. in human psychology."

"Huh, you mean to say people pay him so much just for talking?" Chaddha was shocked as they approached their vehicle. Vayu nodded a yes.

"Then my wife can also earn so much money. *Har waqt bakbak bakbak karti rehti hai,*" Chaddha said enthusiastically.

Vayu burst out laughing.

Abhimanyu opened the door of his flat in a hurry, rushed to the dining table and poured out all the things he had stolen from Oorja's house. His hands fumbled on those papers and photographs to find Yusuf Malik and Suraj Kumar. And he detected them quite effortlessly as Oorja had written names behind each of those photographs. He took pictures of both the photographs in his mobile and sent them to Chakra, typing their name below the pictures.

A message popped up on his mobile almost immediately – '*Thoda waqt lagega.*'

He kept the photographs of a few syndicate members in his locker, threw the rest of the photographs and documents in a metal bucket in the bathroom, and poured kerosene on them. He had to return to the dining table from the bathroom as he heard the ring of his mobile.

"Good morning sir," he greeted, receiving the call from DGP, Omprakash Bakshi.

"Abhi, I am withdrawing your suspension as I want you to expedite your investigation on the Shanaya murder case. It's a very sensitive case, and both the police department and government are under huge pressure until we get closer. I just had a discussion with the forensic team too. They must be ready with their report in a day or two," Omprakash informed.

"Thank you, sir. You won't be disappointed," Abhimanyu replied.

"This is your last chance, Abhi. All your recklessness can be forgiven if you crack this case." Omprakash admonished him before disconnecting the call.

Abhimanyu sighed in relief, drew his pouch of tablets from the pocket and mashed one of the tablets to dust, pressing his thumb against it on the palm. He poured that dust on the dining table, separated it into four strips before snorting them. He spent an hour on that chair, basking his dopey trip, and walked towards the bathroom to finish his job. He felt as if something hammered the core of his senses, and he stumbled over the floor. He grabbed the curtain of a nearby window to get back his balance. However, the knobs of the drapery rod couldn't bear his weight and he fell on the floor with the drape and the rod. After spending a few seconds lying on the floor, he raised himself. He reached his chest-pocket, pulled out his aviator, and covered his eyes to avoid the illuminated vision around him and reached the bathroom lurching.

He reached the pocket of his jeans to grab the lighter, brought it out, and pressed it to trigger a tiny flame. As he kneeled by that metal bucket to set those papers and photographs on fire, a gusty wind extinguished the flame of his lighter. He felt the presence of a human spirit behind him. He turned back in a hurry to witness that bluish-green pair of eyes.

"Ahi," he whispered.

Abhimanyu saw Ahi standing just behind him like a goddess, glowing from within. Few long locks of her short hair were floating in the wind, falling on her forehead and eyes sometimes. She smiled, stretching her rosy lips, which made a pair of deep dimples on her cheeks.

She leaned close to his face and asked softly, "Why are you helping them? You have all the proofs in your possession to destroy the syndicate forever. Why are you not handing them over to the higher authorities? Don't you love me anymore? Have you forgotten your promise, love?"

"No, love! I haven't," Abhimanyu muttered. After a moment of silence, he chuckled and said, "They are much stronger than these papers and photographs. Our law and order can't touch them; they distort law for their benefit. If any investigation starts based on these proofs, they will cut the link that could connect them with any crime and fly away from India. Or they will buy the whole judicial system."

Abhimanyu took his aviators off, looked at Ahi's eyes and whispered, "And nobody will find my dead body tomorrow."

She took his face in her hands, traced his cheekbones and jaw line with her fingers and asked, "Do you want to live without me?"

Abhimanyu grabbed her soft palm on his cheek and whispered, "I have to… until I kill them all. And till then, I can't afford to blow off my cover. I must be one of them to destroy them; it's not possible as an outsider. They are much stronger than me."

Ahi kissed his forehead. He felt a hollowness inside his brain as his eyelids became too heavy to lift. He felt an ultimate impuissance just before fainting on the floor.

Chaddha urged Vayu to halt and have breakfast on the way to Poonam's place. But Vayu was in a hurry to complete the interrogation of the direct and obvious suspect pool of Shanaya's case. Even the tempting offer of hot idli-sambar from an authentic South Indian restaurant couldn't weaken his determination. Compelled by the situation, Chaddha rushed his SUV to the destination of their tentatively last interrogation.

Both were quiet until Vayu asked, "Chaddha ji, what's your opinion about Abhimanyu?"

They exchanged a glance. Chaddha took a few more mute moments to open his mouth and say, "He is the brightest star of our department. Youngest DCP, the most decorated officer in NCR and a great human being. I have learnt a lot from him."

Vayu chuckled, turning his face away from Chaddha, looked outside the windows and whispered, "The eye sees only what the mind is prepared to comprehend."

"*Hanji?*" Chaddha was surprised.

"Nothing, it's a quote by Robertson Davies."

There was a brief silence inside their vehicle except for the noise of the engine before Vayu asked, "So, why did the best cop of this universe become so drastic, irresponsible, irascible and addicted?"

Vayu's sarcasm was sharp enough to make Chaddha sullen while he replied, "Like that Abhimanyu in Mahabharata, our Abhimanyu also got trapped in the *chakravyuha* of life."

Silence overwhelmed everything once again.

"Vayu, how would you behave if you lost someone you loved more than yourself? For whom you could go to any extent, just to see a smile on their face. With whom you want to spend the rest of your life with?" Chaddha asked musingly.

Chaddha asked again, having no response from Vayu, "What does your research on human psychology and behaviour say?"

"Of course, grief would be the common emotional state of mind, but the behaviour or the process of coping with that misery depends on individual perceptions. Every person uses three lenses to see, comprehend and experience any incident – facts and data; choices and preferences; and the wholeness of relationship and similar things. Now, the usage of these lenses varies from person to person," Vayu explained, making a lot of hand gestures in the air.

"What about those people who don't use spectacles, like you and me?" Chaddha asked, stealing a glance of Vayu in between his driving.

Vayu stared at Chaddha blankly for some moments and muttered, "They can use sunglasses."

Chaddha nodded thoughtfully.

"*Bhenchod*," Chaddha murmured, aggressively pressing the brake to avoid a collision with a bike. The traffic on the road had increased exponentially with the progression of the day.

"So, was that a breakup? I...I mean, how did he lose the love of his life?" Vayu seemed uncomfortable while asking that personal question about Abhimanyu as that was none of his business.

"She was murdered. Her parents accused Abhi as her killer and launched a case against him. I heard that they had some proof against Abhi as well. But I don't believe them. Abhi can kill himself for Ahi, but he can't ever harm her; killing is beyond my imagination. They were made for each other," Chaddha informed in a soft voice, concentrating on his driving as if he was talking to himself.

"But that proof must not be strong enough to arrest him," Vayu commented.

"It's an audio recording which proves Abhi's involvement; quite a strong evidence. But the department decided not to arrest him until the closure of the case, as he is one of the most rewarded officers." Concern was evident in Chaddha's voice. "We met Ahi for the first time during our investigation of Devang Awasthi's murder. She had magical bluish-green eyes which were out of this world. I had never seen such eyes before. She was not only beautiful but also intelligent enough to help us in our investigation with that manuscript. And I am sure those people only killed her and framed our innocent Abhimanyu," Chaddha continued under one breath, then paused for a moment and added, "They were about to marry, and Ahi had come to Noida for...."

Vayu interrupted, "Which manuscript are you talking about?"

"There was a manuscript written by Devang Awasthi, where he exposed a few powerful and influential people of NCR. Devang himself was a part of their group. So, he was aware of all minute details of that group and its illegal businesses," Chaddha said, taking a sharp turn into a narrow alley.

"And Ahi was a journalist who had managed to get that manuscript and wanted to publish their name? Is that the case?" Impatient Vayu asked as Chaddha was mute while carefully tackling his metallic giant on the wheel through that narrow lane.

"No! Ahi was a publisher; she wanted to publish that as a book," Chaddha concluded as he parked the SUV in front of the single storied house and announced, "This should be Poonam's home according to the address."

Chaddha turned off the ignition and hopped out of the vehicle.

"How are you so sure that she was killed because of that manuscript?' Vayu enquired as he got off too.

"The night she was killed in Noida, someone set fire to her office in Kolkata and burnt everything to ashes. Isn't it obvious?" Chaddha informed as they walked towards Poonam's house.

"I see! Do we have a copy of that manuscript by chance? Aren't we investigating that case anymore?" Vayu asked like a curious kid.

Chaddha shook his head and informed, "No! We are not pursuing that case anymore. The department declared us incompetent for that case as we are emotionally attached to the victim and handed over the case to a few officers who are close to Ahi's father, DGP of Kolkata, Dhritiman Chatterjee."

They reached in front of the door and Vayu pressed the doorbell.

"Can't we contact anyone who used to work in Ahi's publication?" Vayu wasn't ready to give up.

"I don't know any of her colleagues," Chaddha replied instantly. Then on second thoughts, he added with a mischievous smile, "But I have someone in that investigating team who might help us get some contacts." Vayu grinned like a thrilled Cheshire cat.

The door opened partly, and a mesmerizing face peeped through it. Vayu stood there in awestricken silence, witnessing her striking resembles with Shanaya. Except the hair, she was a clone of her stepsister.

"Can we speak to Poonam Nischol?" Chaddha finally asked after a few awkward silent moments, compelled by the situation. Vayu had turned into a mannequin and kept staring at Poonam.

Poonam had long wavy hair like those ripples on the tranquil surface of a pond. A few of her wavy locks covered her forehead above a pair of slender and arching eyebrows. As if her fair complexion, a pair of starched, dark-brown and dreamy eyes just above the mounted cheekbones, long eyelashes, a sharp nose, and thin rosy lips were not enough to spellbind a male. She also had a dimple on her chin in between a pair of well-defined jaw lines and a faint and tiny mole at the edge of her lower lips, which had been playing hide and seek as she moved her lips. Red, green and yellow paints haphazardly kissed her face and throat. She was looking like a doll in her white vest top and denim shorts.

"Yes, it's me," Poonam replied speculatively.

"We are investigating the case of your sister's murder, and we need your help to answer a few of our questions," Vayu replied, flashing his ID.

Poonam invited them inside her house and led them to a small drawing-room. It was a flat of two rooms, one kitchen, one bathroom, and a drawing-room.

"Have you arrested anyone yet?" she asked, making some space for them to sit on a couple of beanbags as their existence was hidden under the piles of canvases of various sizes, rags, and newspapers.

Countless bottles of turpentine, tubes and cans of oil paints, palettes, uncountable brushes of different shapes and sizes, pencils and a few easels were scattered on the floor. One large canvas of an unfinished painting was kept on an easel at the corner, near the window along with a stool where few brushes, a palette, one rag, few tubes of oil paint and brushes were arranged neatly. The air inside the house was filled with the smell of turpentine and oil paints.

"Not yet," Chaddha replied, staring at those beanbags in discomfort. He glanced over the entire drawing room for a chair as he could imagine his uneasiness while sitting on those low beanbags, twisting his legs and bulky tummy.

She gestured them to have a seat.

"I am fine here," Chaddha announced and stood, resting his back on the nearest wall.

Poonam smiled, reading Chaddha's contorted face, brought a chair for him from one of the rooms, and asked, "Is this okay?" Chaddha nodded, grinning.

"Is that your current work?" Vayu asked, pointing to the largest canvas near the window and reclined comfortably on one of the beanbags.

Poonam retorted, occupying another beanbag, "I don't think that's the question you are looking answers for. Can we come to the point?"

Vayu adjusted his posture to observe every minute expression on Poonam's face during their conversation and asked, "How was your relation with your elder sister?" After a tiny pause, he added, "Rather, it will be better to say stepsister."

She glowered at Vayu for a moment before whispering, "She was my world!"

Vayu observed her stretched and eloquent pair of eyes, glittering beneath a layer of tears; they were innocent, hurt and honest.

Poonam continued while playing with the ring in her thumb, "Di used to be busy all the time for her business, other social and charitable work. But every week, according to my convenience, she kept one day absolutely free. Except me, no one could reach her on those escape days."

Vayu noticed her face light up in pride.

Poonam told, chortling, "We used to hang out on those entire days, sharing the slices of our lives; we had a rule of not keeping any secrets between us. We had watched countless movies together; she was a big fan of Chris Evan. My all-time favourite is Leonardo DiCaprio, and we always bickered over them for pleasure."

The Sinful Silence • 93

Few tiny, small red spots on her right forearms couldn't escape Vayu's eyes. He glued his eyes on her right arm to comprehend the source of those spots.

"So, why were you staying separately from your Di?" Vayu asked, noticing a few marks of wounds on her right wrist, but her left arm had neither any spots nor wounds.

"I need my own space for this chaos," she replied, pointing towards those piles of paintings and all kinds of arty stuff scattered on the floor. "And a lot of me time for my creative work. She had done her job to raise me up, and I didn't want to disturb Di. Moreover, I am a grown-up, educated, and independent woman now to live on my own. There is no other..."

"Are you left-handed?" Vayu enquired, cutting her words.

"What?... Why?... Yes, I am," she frowned and asked, "If you are not interested in listening to me then, why are you wasting my time asking questions?"

Vayu smiled and answered, "Believe me, I am all ears. But I have to cut you short when you are going off the track due to time constraints."

"Huh! How is my being a lefty relevant to Di's murder?" she snapped back.

"Not directly, but that fact reveals a few things about you."

"And what the hell are those things about me?" she almost shrieked, losing her patience on Vayu.

Chaddha became quite uncomfortable as he became acquainted with hair-lipped Vayu in the last few days and he had learnt about the choleric Poonam as well in the last few minutes. He glanced at the exit to prepare his mind to escape.

"You are addicted to drugs and prone to suicide. I was a little sceptical about those spots and scars on your right hand. But your clean left hand and your confirmation of being a lefty made it clear to me," Vayu commented with his usual ease, surprising Chaddha. Poonam was mute.

"How or why did you become a drug addict, and why did you try to kill yourself?" Vayu asked calmly. He leaned towards Poonam, took a close look at her wrist, and said, "Three suicide attempts, to be more precise."

Gloom cast a shadow on her bright face while she smirked before answering Vayu, "There is no particular answer of your why and how. I am just cursed to be born with anxiety issues. I have been suffering from depression and irascibility syndromes from childhood. I had started taking drugs during my college days to keep myself unconscious; that was my escape from all the chaos inside my mind. I used to hate myself the most in this world and tried to kill myself several times; three of those attempts were by slitting my wrist."

Poonam's long eyelashes drenched while she blinked away the tears. A drop of tear rolled down on her pinkish cheek and halted between her lips. She wiped it with her fingers and continued, "Di said that Mummy was ill while delivering me, and that might be the reason for my issues. Di was always there with me like a banyan tree; tolerated all my illogical tantrums, rescued me from all my self-destructive attempts, boosted my self-esteem and taught me to love myself first."

"I see! So, how are you doing now?" Vayu enquired.

"Good!" She nodded in confidence, and after a thoughtful pause, she said, "Di had helped me find a constructive outlet for all the negative thoughts trapped inside my brain." She pointed at those canvases.

"That's interesting! So, painting is kind of a meditation for you, not your profession."

Her lips broke into a small smile. "Yes, and no. Initially, I started painting for seeking peace for my soul. However, gradually it became my profession when people started buying the paintings."

Poonam stood up, gestured at them to wait, went inside her bedroom and returned with a small card.

"I am not sure if a cop will be interested in paintings and stuff. But I would like to invite both of you to my next painting exhibition," she said, handing over that card to Vayu.

Vayu had a glimpse at that card, smiled, slipped it in his pocket and said, "Sure! Can I have a look at your paintings, if you don't mind?"

Poonam smiled, softly biting the tip of her tongue apologetically and mumbled, "Please."

Vayu started randomly lifting some canvases from the piles on the floor; most of them were incomplete.

"Check there," she suggested, pointing at a few canvases kept with earnest attention, unlike others on a small table.

Their discussion elongated for a few more hours over coffee before Vayu and Chaddha stepped out of her house. There was a pleasant assurance in Vayu's mind to exclude Poonam from his suspect list.

On the way back to the police station, Vayu bought a large corkboard, few colourful threads, few board pins, a bunch of sticky notes and a box of coloured pencils. That provoked Chaddha to behave like a curious kid as he had never seen such stationeries being used to solve any homicide case in his forty-five years of service. However, Chaddha couldn't manage any word other than "Investigation-board" from Vayu, even after asking several questions.

Chaddha tagged along like a rat behind the Pied Piper of Hamelin when Vayu rushed towards his desk. Vayu fastened that corkboard on the wall opposite his desk and pinned a portrait of Shanaya in the middle of it. Chaddha stood in awestricken silence behind Vayu, gazing at the board. One by one, Vayu pinned the portraits of Rizwan, Jignesh, Sandy and Supriya at the top of the board and turned back to find all his colleagues huddled, staring at the board.

"Chaddha ji, I need the picture of Shanaya's husband Manoj, and that psychologist, Dr Rahul Khanna. Google it, you will definitely find them," Vayu instructed, pulling out a red colour thread from the bag where all other stationeries were kept.

Chaddha nodded and murmured, "Investigation board!" and departed for his desk to access his computer.

Vayu cut the red thread into four pieces, tied one end of each to the pin on Shanaya's portrait, and another end to the pin on the rest of the pictures on the board. In the meanwhile, Chaddha brought the prints of pictures of Manoj and Rahul.

"This is the front picture on his website. Just look at him! *Buddhe mein* swag *hai*," Chaddha remarked, pointing at Rahul's picture where he was posing on an ornamented chair in a designer kurta, pyjama and shawl. Like a king.

"And this guy has only one picture, that too with Shanaya; it's from some newspaper. Lucky guy got a chance to show his face in the newspaper just because of his famous wife," Chaddha passed his judgment.

"Famous wife of a common man; that's a strong angle along with his financial crunch. Superb, Chaddha ji," Vayu appreciated, pinning those two pictures at the bottom of the board and connected them with Shanaya's picture using two pieces of red threads.

Chaddha beamed with a proud smile, glancing over the faces of his colleagues.

"May I come in, sir?" A husky voice asked in a pseudo-polite tone.

All the policemen who had been enjoying that colourful investigation board rushed away to their desks on hearing Abhimanyu's voice.

"Take off that board from the wall immediately. Vayu and Chaddha ji, let's have a discussion," Abhimanyu ordered while calling them towards his cabin.

Vayu and Chaddha exchanged a look, took that board down to the floor from the wall and followed him. Abhimanyu gestured at them to grab chairs for themselves as they entered his cabin. He climbed on his desk, hopping.

"What's that board about?" he asked, adjusting the bandage on his forearm.

"That's the investigation board of Mrs Shanaya Mehta's murder case," Vayu replied immediately. Chaddha grinned like a proud team-man.

"Are you out of your mind? This is real life, not a Hollywood movie; and this building is a public police station in India, not some FBI or CIA headquarter. Anyone can walk in at any time. We can't hang pictures of real people on the wall for public display as the suspects of murder until it's proven in court." Abhimanyu's voice had been climbing to a new level of loudness with each sentence.

He continued, "Moreover, if someone from the media comes to know about it, we will be screwed. It's a significant investigation for the government; the Opposition has created huge pressure on the government and the police department. This case has become one of the decisive factors in the upcoming election. We can't afford any mistake. Is that clear?"

Chaddha nodded like an obedient kid.

"We have already made a pointless mistake which could have been easily avoided in the first place. Beating up a journalist," Vayu retorted softly.

"What?" Abhimanyu yelled.

"*Jo ho gaya, so ho gaya*! We can't change that now. Let's discuss the case; we have completed our interrogations of all the suspects," Chaddha interfered, diverting the topic.

"Do we have any strong evidence or witness or confession which could lead us to make an arrest?" Abhimanyu asked Chaddha, glowering at Vayu.

"Come on, Abhimanyu! Don't tell me that you are expecting an arrest within one and a half days for a complicated murder mystery like this," Vayu raised his voice a little louder this time.

Abhimanyu bent over from the table and whispered close to Vayu's ear, "Call me sir. I am your DCP."

Vayu turned his face away from him, surly.

The atmosphere in the room had turned quite uncomfortable for Chaddha. He took a gulp of air to steady himself and intervened, "We should work as a team now. Let's talk about the case. We have a lot of stuff to wrap up, and no time at all."

"Chaddha ji, you are a senior constable. You should have stopped him, instead of involving in his filmy ventures," Abhimanyu criticised.

Chaddha apologised, bending his head down.

After a few moments of silence, Abhimanyu asked, "So, who all are there in our suspect list?"

"Four of her close friends attended her birthday party – Rizwan, Jignesh, Sandy and Supriya; her husband Manoj; her psychologist Rahul Khanna, and her sister Poonam," Chaddha informed.

"Poonam is innocent. We can take her out from our suspect list," Vayu remarked.

Abhimanyu and Chaddha turned their face toward Vayu, who explained, "I didn't find any motive for Poonam to kill her kind, warm and nurturing step-sister whom she had been completely depending on since her birth. Poonam realises that fact very well. There is no financial dispute between the sisters. Moreover, I couldn't read anything suspicious in her facial expressions during our conversation."

"I do know a bit of profiling too. Choosing the word 'conversation' instead of 'interrogation' speaks about your favouritism which could jeopardise our investigation," Abhimanyu said, rubbing the bandage on his head to scratch the itchy wound beneath it. He frowned in annoyance, realising that he had to revisit the doctor.

"Include Poonam in our suspect list," Abhimanyu ordered.

Chaddha patted on Vayu's thigh, noticing the disappointment on his face.

Abhimanyu got down from the table with a light leap, walked around the table to reach his chair at the other side, lounged himself on it and inquired, "Who has the strongest motive among these suspects?"

"Her husband, Manoj Sharma – a broke stock gambler who had given up on his dream of becoming a singing sensation long ago. He borrowed a huge amount from local usurer with high interest to pay back the bank debt and lately he had no other option but borrow money from his wife, Shanaya. Obviously, this wouldn't be the first time that he is in this situation," Vayu explained, gathering his peace of mind as he didn't want to botch up the first case of his career for vengeance against an insane senior.

"So, Shanaya might have refused to help him after his repetitive act to borrowing money, and he killed his wife," Abhimanyu concluded.

"Yes, he had been receiving threats from local goons. Moreover, inferiority complex and jealousy also could be the motives," Vayu added.

Abhimanyu nodded thoughtfully and asked, "What about Rizwan? What could his possible motive be?"

"Revenge! Because she slapped him in front of other guests and they broke up years ago," Chaddha re-joined the discussion, smiling proudly.

Vayu shook his head in disagreement and said, "No, that doesn't sound strong enough. He broke the relationship, not Shanaya, and murdering an ex because of slapping publicly, doesn't make sense to me." After a thoughtful silence, Vayu continued, "In that perspective, Jignesh has the strongest motive among her close friends. Shanaya had refused his proposal, slapped and insulted him in front of his classmates, and her ex-boyfriend Rizwan had abused him brutally. And that incident overwhelmed him so deeply that he stopped coming to college. It was Jignesh who arranged this reunion on Shanaya's birthday."

"I see!" Abhimanyu mumbled and asked, "And what about the other two of her friends?"

"Supriya has a stronger motive than Sandy because she had one-sided feelings of love and admiration for Rizwan. But after her interrogation, I felt that she had moved on long back. And Sandy has no strong motive to kill Shanaya. She had refused to invest in one of his animation projects. If it's not a mere accident driven by his sudden anger outburst, he is innocent," Vayu explained with a lot of enthusiasm.

"And her psychiatrist, Rahul Khanna," Chaddha interfered.

"He is a psychologist, not a psychiatrist. Vayu corrected Chaddha and continued, "We just had a short conversation with him, and I didn't see any reason to suspect him as of now. However, we must keep him in touch for our reference to know more about Shanaya's adolescence other than her college life. We had to trick him into getting hold of some CDs, which contain Shanaya's therapy sessions. He was looking for a court order which we must arrange before his advocate knocks at our door."

"I am on it," Chaddha assured.

"But right now, we can't arrest any of these suspects due to lack of solid evidence or witness. Am I correct?" Abhimanyu asked, reclining on his chair.

Vayu and Chaddha nodded, agreeing to the fact.

"If we get the report from the forensics department, we can narrow the suspect pool further, or in the best-case scenario, we might identify the killer as well," Vayu sounded confident.

Abhimanyu laughed for a moment and teased, "Mr FBI, this is India. We don't get forensic help in all cases unless it's a case like Shanaya Mehta's murder, the highly escalated one. Because forensic tests are quite expensive. What will you do in other normal cases?"

Vayu was silent.

"Sir, in other cases, we don't have this kind of time crunch, right?" Chaddha interfered to support Vayu.

"We are getting enough time, Chaddha ji," Abhimanyu retorted leaving his chair and walked towards Vayu. He bent over Vayu's face and whispered, "Provided, you concentrate more on the investigation than complaining about your senior."

Chaddha stared at Vayu in shock while Abhimanyu walked away towards the exit. Abhimanyu turned back, reaching the door and ordered, "I need this investigation to be documented in detail by tomorrow. We must show some progress to our higher authority. Otherwise, they will hand over this case to CBI, and that would be shameful for us."

"Did you…co…complain? About the encounter that… that night!" Chaddha asked, fumbling in disbelief immediately after Abhimanyu left the room.

Vayu nodded while he started to rise from his chair.

"But why, Vayu?" Chaddha asked, grabbing Vayu's wrist from behind as he attempted to leave the room.

Vayu turned his face and screamed, "Because I think that was the right thing to do. I can't allow someone to use law and order of my country for his sadistic pleasures and jokes."

Chaddha had never seen Vayu that angry before; it startled him to silence.

"I am sorry, Chaddha ji, but my country and its laws are most important for me." Vayu's eyes, face and voice were soaked in patriotism.

Vayu stormed out of the cabin. Chaddha kept standing there, baffled.

It was quite late in the night when Vayu returned to his flat after completing the documentation of his investigation. He had to buy a packet of sliced bread while returning because all the restaurants near his apartment were closed. He toasted six slices of bread with butter after freshening up. He returned to his drawing-room carrying those pieces of bread on a plate, placed it on the hand-rest of the couch, fetched out that pack of CDs that he had taken from Dr Rahul, and played the first CD on his TV.

Vayu felt it thrilling to watch Shanaya breathing and moving, though she was on the television screen. She looked stunning in her bottle-green business suit and skirt on a white shirt. She was sitting on one of those two red couches in Rahul's office. Vayu was optimistic about finding some information regarding her life between absconding from college and marriage and her pregnancy.

"Will you record our conversation? Shouldn't it be private?" she asked, looking at the camera.

She had a heavy voice and an unhurried way of speaking; tranquil, fearless, and confident. Her voice was breaking at the end of each sentence and sounded like a low humming chorus of two women. Other than hair and aging effects, the voice was another attribute that could differentiate her from Poonam.

"That's for my reference; it won't be disclosed to anyone. It is difficult, you know, to remember my conversation with all the clients. So, I refresh myself before each visit with my clients."

It was not difficult for Vayu to identify that low, husky, thunderous and rumbling voice, wrapped in British dialect.

"Client?" Shanaya giggled, covering her mouth. "Was that a sugar coating on the word patient?" Shanaya asked, hanging a smile at the corner of her thin shiny lips, which were covered under a soft-pink lip-gloss.

Rahul laughed and said, "Not really, and I mean it. Being a psychologist, I can't label anyone as "mental"; it's just different perceptions of human psychology." He asked after a tiny pause, "Have you heard about lip-plates?'

Her tiny and dangling diamond earrings sparkled with the movement of her head as she shook her head in a 'no'.

"There are few tribal groups in Africa, like Mursi, Chai and Tirma, who wear wooden plates in their lower lips. A girl's lower lip is cut by her mother or by another woman when she reaches the age of fifteen or sixteen. The cut is held open by a wooden plug until the wound heals. They stretch that cut by inserting progressively larger plugs over several months and wear a comparatively decorated wooden plate as the opening of the lower lip reaches to the desired diameter. Moreover, it is the teenage girls' choice to have their lips pierced and not something older women or men force upon them. What's your opinion about this?"

His voice sounded like a piece of music to Vayu.

"Apparently, it seems insanity, but I believe they must have some significant reason to tolerate the pain. Isn't it?" She responded, arranging her side locks behind the ear.

"Exactly! According to them, it is a 'bridge' between the individual and society - between the biological 'self' and the social 'self'!"

"What if someone fails to create that bridge between the biological 'self' and social 'self'?" she asked slowly in a soft and deep voice. Her eyes were moist.

"Nothing is wrong in that, provided that person is happy being oneself." After a silent moment, Dr Rahul asked, "How are you doing, Shanaya? Why are we here today?"

"I am addicted, but not ashamed of it," she whispered.

"What kind of addiction is it? Drugs? Or alcohol? Or…"

Shanaya interrupted before he could finish his sentence, "Humans. The strongest drug that exists for a human is another human. Isn't it?"

Vayu couldn't hear any response from Rahul. However, Shanaya's facial expression suggested his unanimity.

"I am a nymphomaniac; at least that's the word which describes me as per our society," she replied and asked, smirking. "I wonder, whether this patriarchal society has even thought of any similar word for males as well."

"It's there. Satyriasis, a man with excess sexual desire. Why do you think that you are addicted to humans, or sex, rather?"

She voiced reluctantly, "I…I masturbate." Her eyes flickered in embarrassment.

"Go on, I am listening, and don't hesitate. Imagine you are alone in this room and talking to yourself in front of a mirror. I am your mirror."

She continued, but her hesitation had not gone completely, "I masturbate several times in a day. In fact, whenever I get some free hours, it gets the best of me, and I do it repetitively, twice or even thrice at a stretch. Predominantly it's porn, but sometimes my imaginative scenarios drag me to the edge of arousal. I am that miserable, anxious mess of a woman who loves to spend time alone in her dark bedroom, balancing the hot laptop between her necked thighs, scrolling for hours to select the perfect porn according to her mood, watching them in low volume or plugging the earphones and savours elongated orgasmic pleasure in the same wet spot on the bed."

"And how do you choose them? I mean, what are your criteria to select porn? Soft and romantic, rough and sadistic, or the anatomic features of the actors?"

"It depends on my mood at that moment," she answered without wasting a second to think.

"And what about your imaginative scenarios or fantasies?"

"Well…There is a pattern in those contents; whether it's porn or my fantasy," Shanaya replied after a while, leafing some memories and added, "All of them are based on some twisted relationship like a teenage schoolgirl fucking her stepdad on the kitchen counter while her mom showers upstairs or a horny mother fucking the friend of her son in between their group study."

The tip of her nose and ears turned red as she said, "Lately, I have discovered that females are equally appealing to me. I fantasise more of being intimate with a chubby married woman, cuddling her in my arms, watching her tremble as I touch her between her legs, those goosebumps on her breast, the hardened nipples. But I don't know how I can reach the climax with her. So, I twist my imagination that her husband catches us red-handed and rapes me as a punishment in front of his wife."

A silence lasted about a minute before Shanaya told, smiling, "Now, I believe it's easy for you to label me with a lot of words – insane, addicted or dirty. Isn't it?"

"Not at all. If I can't call the excess appetite for food as insanity, how can I say that excess appetite for sex is madness? But, excess of anything has a negative impact," Rahul asked after a pause, "Are you noticing any lack of concentration, anxiety or irritation while you are in office?"

"No," Shanaya said.

"Are you ashamed of your habits or feeling guilty?"

"Yes, a guilt of not feeling any guilt. You know, Doc, I am ashamed of my business," she told softly, wiping her moist eyes, and continued. "I, as a businesswoman, exploit innocent people and loot their money. Humans' social behaviour is restricted to emotions; fear, envy, jealousy, pride, prestige, sadness and happiness. Not all these emotions work for all kinds of people. So, these companies categorise them based on their emotional buttons and press them to sell their products."

"Go on, I am listening."

"Fear is our friend as it helps us to prevent any danger in the future. Especially for middle-class people, fear is an inevitable trigger point. Hence, these companies just scare them with some unpleasant consequences if they don't buy their products, causing them to spend more than their real needs. Envy is the trigger point for the young and immature people. We just need to hire some celebrities to lure them. That's the easiest market. You can sell shit using celebrity faces. Sometimes we pretend that we are selling happiness, but we just squeeze their sadness and sell expensive delusive hopes; fairness creams, slimming pills and a hell lot of similar shit. We even intervene in their privacy, buying historical data of their purchase and bombard their devices with similar products."

"Wow! That's deep social profiling," Vayu murmured in admiration with a mouthful of bread.

Shanaya reclined on the cushioned hand rest and said, sighing, "I do a lot of charities to just console myself from this guilt of cheating innocent people."

"Now I know why you are the youngest achiever of so many prestigious business awards," Rahul appreciated.

Vayu paused the video as his phone rang, displaying Dubey's number.

"What's up, Dubey ji?" Vayu asked, receiving the call.

"Vayu, you must have heard of a lady's murder in a motel by the highway. I have reached a dead-end while investigating the case. I need your help here." Dubey sounded worried.

"Okay, give me some background."

"A female victim strangled to death, named Oorja Shah. Twenty-eight years old according to her voter card. We haven't found anything other than that voter card in her belongings. We have cross-checked every database. She has no mobile phone, credit card, driving license, pan card, bank account or any document that could get us her whereabouts or any background. We contacted the nearest police station of her village, according to the address on her voter card. But no one lives there."

"Hmm... So, someone murdered a ghost," Vayu mumbled.

"Yes."

"Absence of driving license... implies that she used to commute by public transportation. So, start enquiring all the drivers of autos, buses and cars near that motel, except those vehicles which operate under any web application-based transportation company, as she had no SIM as well," Vayu advised, taking time between his words to think.

"Thanks Vayu!"

"And Dubey ji, stay alert and safe! You have touched something big and mighty. Her ghostly lifestyle doesn't seem like a coincidence to me. It's a conscious effort. In this era of cheap technologies and convenience, if she had chosen to live like an ancient species, there must be some reason behind it. And keep me posted," Vayu warned.

"Sure." Dubey disconnected the call.

Vayu resumed the video.

"Help me to understand, Shanaya, why are we here today, discussing your life? If you don't feel guilty for your addiction, then it's absolutely fine. And I don't think you are here for me to convince you to quit your business, right?"

"No, I am here for Manoj, my husband. Lately, he has discovered my obsession, which made him quite depressed. He doesn't talk to me much, except for a few words. He is a beautiful singer, you know. Not so famous as he has only one flop album. But every night, when I used to return home after prolonged and tiring office hours, he used to sing for me, and I listened to his voice for hours before falling asleep, resting my head on his lap."

She sounded in some other zone while talking about her husband, staring outside the window. Her voice was soft and low, her eyes moist. Vayu had to increase the volume to hear her out clearly.

"I have hurt that innocent man who loves me more than I love myself. I am ashamed of turning him into a living mummy," she whispered.

"So, you mean to say that he is upset because you watch porn and masturbate? However, I believe most of us do or used to do that. He might be worried about your health, both physically and mentally, as the excess practice of onanism has depressing consequences."

"Tell me about it," Shanaya told sighing as she tapped a handkerchief below her eyes to soak the tears.

Vayu could see Dr Khanna's right hand on the screen while he placed a glass of water on the table in front of Shanaya.

Shanaya picked up the glass, sipped the water and continued, "My obsession has not restricted within my dark bedroom anymore. There are men in my life who I don't know personally but have slept with. Sometimes, I have driven for miles at midnight just to fuck a stranger. Even my cognizance of unknown danger couldn't stop my feet. I could have been robbed, blackmailed, exploited, gang-raped, tortured, murdered, or my identity would have been exploited. But believe me, all those practical parameters seemed insignificant compared to that hunger in my core, that thirst to be touched, the craving of a strong and rough hand all over my body, that pain of soft bites and tight grasp, and that thrill of fornication."

"So, basically, you're bored of your conjugal life and longing for some adventures? Or is there any incapability in your husband?"

"No, I am not bored with him at all, and he is quite potent and healthy. But I don't feel sexual attraction for him," Shanaya snapped back, frowning.

"Why don't you guys have a peaceful discussion and go for a mutual divorce? We shouldn't drag a relationship if it has lost its charm; it will jeopardise both of your lives in the long run," he suggested.

"He has no one except me; no earning as well, and that might be his reason to tolerate my boisterousness silently. Moreover, we can't live without each other. If I don't see him at home after returning from work, I feel so empty. His singing is like a lullaby to me; I can't sleep without it. It absorbs all my fatigues, tensions and emptiness. I love him." Her voice shivered.

"I think you are confused between two of your emotions – love and kindness. You feel sympathy for your husband, not love, and have created a cloud in your mind about his singing and stuff. Loyalty comes from love and respect, but kindness..."

"Loyalty?" She laughed for a while and continued, "I have seen those happy and loyal couples, not having sex outside their conjugal partners, but after a few years of marriage, turning their backs to their spouse and masturbating, thinking of someone else while sharing the same bed."

"Is that what you call loyalty? I call it hypocrisy," she asked softly after a pause, smirking.

Vayu didn't hear any response from Rahul.

"Doc, why can't we differentiate love from lust? Why can't we accept that we don't need to be sexually attracted to that same person we love? I can die for my husband, but not for those men. I don't give a damn for them," she questioned politely as she kept playing with her necklace.

"Because that's the popular and influential thought of our society – to love and make love to the same human."

After a momentary silence, Rahul declared, "Let's end our first session here."

The screen blacked out for a few seconds before the video of the next session popped up on the screen. Vayu paused the video and went to hit the hay, but the riots in his mind of contradictory thoughts didn't let him sleep. Shanaya's infidelity obviously made her husband a stronger suspect, which was quite satisfactory for Vayu, but her casual flings darkened the case to a mysterious, open-ended precariousness.

"Could any of these men have been the killer?" he whispered, staring at the ceiling fan.

The clock showed 1 a.m. Abhimanyu snorted the first line of cocaine; he felt no effect whatsoever. He went for the second line, snorting deeply, lifted his chin, inhaling the scattered powder on his nostril, and continued until he finished all four lines. The initial buzz lasted for about ten minutes, then he rode out the upshot for about an hour. He always felt an urge to sort another line about fifteen minutes of that first line. Hence, he just sniffed four lines consecutively. He leaned back on the sofa, savouring the emptiness of his head, a state of mind where no pain could touch him, not even the pain of missing Ahi. He wasn't aware of the time he had spent on that couch – awake, idle, no tiny cloud of thoughts, except the vision of those unknown red and white flowers which were printed on Ahi's yellow frock. He could faintly hear an acoustic guitar, a familiar tune, one of his favourites; yeah! Carlos Santana.

"Maria Maria... She reminds me of a west side story," he hummed, smiling.

That guitar became silent for a few seconds before it returned louder to make him realize that his phone was ringing.

"Hello!' he said reluctantly in a sleepy voice. It was an unsaved number.

"Wow! Is that voice of DCP Abhimanyu Rathore? I can't believe it." An overenthusiastic male voice responded.

"May I know who this is?"

"Sir, I am your biggest fan. I heard your name several times on TV, in newspapers and magazines. I know a few of your

The Sinful Silence • 113

investigations, how brilliantly you have solved cases. However, after that incident, my respect for you has increased. What a masterpiece you have created that evening, like a traceless phantom," There was a blend of thrill and admiration in his voice.

"What masterpiece and evening are you talking about? Who are you, by the way?" Abhimanyu enquired in irritation.

"It's obvious for you to forget, after all. You have a lot of responsibilities to take care of. But... but I didn't forget; a die-hard fan of yours, sir. In fact, I have recorded everything to enjoy it, watching repetitively. Sir, I am talking about your work of art at the Drive Inn."

Abhimanyu felt shivers running up and down his spine. That voice had burst the dopiness of his mind to an alarming state.

"Such a clean..."

Abhimanyu interrupted his words, shrieking, "Hey *madarchod*, you don't know what you are playing with." After a pause, he threatened, followed by few finger snaps, "It won't take even an hour for me to trace your location and make you vanish forever."

"Oops! That will endanger your career and life further. Being your biggest fan, I can't allow that to happen. I have scheduled a mail to send the murder footage to a few big media houses and your own police department. So, it's obvious that I am your only key to stop that mail. Even your technical team can't hack my mail ID as they don't have any clue about my email address," he replied.

Abhimanyu kept quiet, finding himself in a most awkward quandary.

"Sir, believe me, I won't let anything happen to you. Please, give me a chance to serve you. My life will become worth living," he pleaded politely.

Abhimanyu found it difficult to control his seething anger as he asked, gnashing, "What the fuck do you want?"

"Correct question! One crore cash only. I know you must be laughing; this amount is not up to your standard. But I will adjust with it," he demanded to wrap his words in dramatic politeness.

"How can I be sure that you won't ask for any more money if I pay you one crore?" Abhimanyu asked as he messaged the number to the cyber-crime department to trace the caller.

"Because you don't have any other option, sir. Do you? Why don't you come to Drive Inn tomorrow, get me the money and finish all this non-sense? Then, you can concentrate on your work without any tension. My name is Mukund."

Abhimanyu was baffled by the confidence of that caller.

"No... no way! Don't plan to kill me because that mail is on the server and only I can stop it. Good night, sir!" Mukund said and disconnected the call.

Abhimanyu kept sitting there, gawking at the screen of his mobile. A message from the cybercrime department popped up on the screen. It had the address of Drive Inn.

Vayu habitually got out of bed earlier than usual. He liked to take control of his to-do list for the day in advance. However, he was quite late to wake up and reach the office that day as he could only catch a few hours of sleep after watching Shanaya's therapy sessions.

Vayu rushed to his desk, thinking of all possible ways to compensate for his delay.

"All of them lied, except Supriya," Chaddha said, dumping a pile of papers on Vayu's desk.

Vayu took a glimpse of that pile and asked, "What do you mean?"

"Rizwan, Sandy and Jignesh had been in touch with Shanaya since the last few years. According to the history of her phone calls and chats, Rizwan was the first to contact her after the final year of their college," Chaddha informed, pulling a chair for himself.

"Excellent! And that tells us we should drop Supriya from our suspect list," Vayu said as his face lit up in immense satisfaction. He was pleased about his correct judgment about Supriya.

"Though she had the strongest motive, being a part of that love-triangle, but that's too outdated and feeble to trigger a strong desire to kill her romantic competitor. I was right," Vayu reassured himself and asked, "What else?"

"Not only that, you are also right about Shanaya's virtual life as well. We got a lot of information from her virtual world to compare to the real one. This Sandy had been blackmailing Shanaya for money. He mentioned some video in the chat and threatened to make it public," Chaddha updated Vayu.

"What kind of video?" Vayu asked frowning, and picked a bunch of papers from the pile on his desk.

"That's not clear from the chat, but it must be something that could endanger Shanaya's reputation for sure."

Vayu nodded thoughtfully, as he hadn't expected something like this coming up.

"We didn't find anything wrong about Jignesh, other than him hiding his continuous communication with Shanaya. He was just trying to convince her to get divorced and marry him," Chaddha said casually.

"But, that's a strong motive to murder; failure and one-sided love," Vayu retorted, glancing through the pages and asked, "And Rizwan?"

"I think Rizwan murdered her. Shanaya was a member of the sports club where Rizwan works as a fitness trainer."

Vayu took his eyes off those pages and looked at Chaddha in surprise.

Chaddha continued reading speculation on Vayu's face, "In few of their chats, Rizwan insulted Shanaya, calling her a characterless whore and cheater. They quarrelled over her intimacy with another trainer named Varun. Rizwan sounded quite jealous of their closeness. However, Shanaya completely ignored him, saying it's her life and none of his business."

Vayu laughed and said, "Our suspects are in a competition to prove their greater suspicion. Now, this Rizwan has almost overtaken Shanaya's husband."

"What about our blackmailer, Sandy?" Chaddha asked.

"I am quite confused about him," Vayu murmured inattentively, riffling through the printed chat histories. He took his eyes off the papers after a few minutes and continued, "It doesn't make sense for him to kill Shanaya as that would permanently end all his chances of getting any money out of her. But I am not sure whether his morbid obsession to accomplish his dream led him to commit the murder out of impulsive anger. Anger makes us mentally impotent." After a thoughtfully pause, he added, "Again, poisoning someone is not an act of impulsive anger; it is a well-planned and organised work of a calm and composed brain."

"I strongly believe that he is not our guy. But he would definitely help to buy us some time and reduce the pressure on us," Vayu remarked smirking.

"How?" Chaddha was quick to ask.

"By arresting him under IPC 503 and 383, for blackmailing and extortion. The department will get something to talk about with the media and higher authorities. Arrange all documents for that," Vayu replied.

"By the way, have we found any dating apps on Shanaya's devices?" Vayu enquired.

"Yes, there were a few of them."

"Make a list of all the people who interacted with her through those apps and sites. It's quite possible that the unsub is none of our current suspects. He could be some random person

Shanaya knew only by their fake name, but had sex with," Vayu instructed while reading those papers.

Chaddha nodded.

An overcrowded, rusted, and partly damaged bus was somehow managing to crawl on the highway towards Badshahpur, a small village of Haryana. Few of the passengers were hanging in the narrow aisle of the bus, holding a greasy, cracked and rustic iron rod that passed throughout the length of the bus. There was an obnoxious smell inside the bus; a mix of smoke, body odour, grease, dust and fading odour of perfume. Yusuf and Suraj were fortunate to have found a seat by a window that was not permanently sealed using cardboard, plastic and ropes, like some other windows.

"*Hum aise chhup chhup ke kyon ji rahe hain*? Why do we have to hide? Neither do we have any criminal record, nor any connection with that girl. Police can't even suspect us," Suraj whispered, leaning his face close to Yusuf's.

Yusuf stared at Suraj frowning, caught a glimpse of the faces around them and gestured at him to shut up. Suraj had an average appearance; skinny, dark brown complexion, a thick moustache covering the upper lips along with salt-and-pepper beard and messy hair. His dirty check shirt, khaki trousers, and bare feet gave him a camouflaged presence, indistinguishable from the mass. On the contrary, Yusuf had a unique appearance with his hazel eyes, light brown hair and beard, extremely fair skin, lean and tall figure, and a scar running through his cheeks.

"*Bhai*, I have a pregnant wife at home. I must be with her now at Jasana. *Humare pas to abhi bohot paisa hai.* Can't we hide in someplace far away along with our families?" Suraj whispered again.

Yusuf glanced around again and murmured, gnashing, "*Mein un thullon se nahi dar raha*," he abused the policemen. "But that lady who gave us the *supari* to kill the girl is too dangerous."

Suraj greened, displaying his yellowish, decayed teeth and told, "*Woh ladki*, Oorja? Are you scared of her?"

"*Abey gandu*! Do you think she is alone? She is just a slave to find some scapegoats like us. That girl, Ahi, was the daughter of DGP of Kolkata. This is something big, and that's why they didn't involve themselves directly and hired us. They must have had a plan to kill us after we completed their work. So that there is no trace that can connect them to Ahi's death. It's easy to kill people like us."

"*Bhenchod*! Why did you agree to do it then, and dragged me in this? I didn't know we had agreed to murder someone. I thought it would be a small smuggling kind of thing. *Mein bhi lalach mein aa gaya tha*," Suraj almost screamed in panic.

Yusuf slapped Suraj, placed his index finger on his lips, and said, whispering, "Shhhh! *Madarchod*! That's why I didn't tell you the truth in the beginning. *Phattu sala*. No one would give us this much money just for smuggling. But I didn't know that it was a contract for murdering the daughter of DGP. *Woh toh kand karne ke baad pata chala*. After a few days, I saw the news of her murder in a newspaper, and everything was written there."

"*Magar, hum toh mar...*" Before Suraj could complete his sentence, Yusuf grabbed his mouth and ordered, "*Bhosdike, ab chup ho ja.*"

Abhimanyu felt the mobile's vibration in his jeans pocket while he kick-started the ignition of his bike. He pulled out the mobile from his pocket and smirked in irritation, glancing at the number.

"Yes?" he responded, frowning.

"Sir, are you coming today? Let's finish this shit quickly. Just one crore. Then you can concentrate on Shanaya Mehta's case without any distraction."

"Give me some time. Minimum ten days. One crore cash is not a joke to arrange," Abhimanyu replied.

"Sir, I am your biggest fan. How can I refuse your proposal? But, ten days are too long to wait, and it's risky too, you know. Let's close the deal in the next seven days. On the eighth day, you will be all over the media," Mukund threatened.

The call got disconnected. After spending a few thoughtful moments, Abhimanyu called one of his colleagues in the cybercrime department.

"I will send you a mobile number after this call. Trace its location 24/7 for the next five days and let me know where it spends most of the time every day," Abhimanyu instructed.

"Sure, sir! Please send the case number along with the phone number."

"Don't worry! I will take care of all the protocol. You just analyse the locations and let me know. Your hard work will be rewarded," Abhimanyu assured before disconnecting the call.

The police department had something to cheer and talk about in front of the media and public after Sandy's arrest.

DGP Omprakash Mishra called for a press conference and announced the new development in the most talked about case in the country.

Jignesh summoned a lawyer for Sandy as a gesture of triumphing over his college friends. His life had reached a stalemate several years back when Shanaya and Rizwan had brutally humiliated him publicly. His thoughts and efforts were triggered to win Shanaya back and please other friends in the pack, isolating Rizwan.

However, Vayu wasn't bothered about Sandy's trial in court as that arrest was just a coin to buy time for the real quest. A few aspects of Shanaya's life were still beyond Vayu's comprehension. He was quite optimistic that the recordings of Shanaya's therapy sessions would enlighten him about her pregnancy and her absconding college. Hence, he resumed the video.

"Let's talk about your childhood. When did you experience any sexual feeling in you for the first time?" Dr Khanna asked Shanaya.

"I am not sure whether it was for the very first time, but that memory is still vivid in my mind," Shanaya told in her usual unhurried way of speaking and smiled.

"I had a friend, Ayesha – a Muslim girl who was compelled to wear a burqa. Whatever might be the reason for her family to cover her under that tent – whether to express her piousness, her sexual modesty, her rejection of western sexuality, to restrict her mobility or for her protection in our male-dominated society – she made a world of self-gratification inside that black boundary. That was an adolescent phase of our lives, you know when we all experienced the drastic changes in our body and explored them in our own way. One day, when I reached school, Ayesha took me to the stairway near the roof. Nobody used to go there as the roof always remained closed, and that was our place to talk dirty. She was thrilled to explain her new discovery of masturbation that didn't need any self-touch, which was a big impediment for our fantasy. I had returned home early that day, making an excuse of my sickness to try that innovative self-orgasm."

She became quiet for a moment, smiled, and asked, "You know what, I love your profession. I mean, getting money to enjoy the secrets of others. Wonderful, isn't it?"

Vayu heard the doctor laughing.

"We didn't have any bathtub or water tank inside our bathroom. So, I had to seal the only outlet on the floor to store the water. I still remember that chillness on my warm kneecaps pressed up against the bathroom's damp wall to position myself under the faucet. I swung open the tap, letting the steady stream of warm water plummet down that untouched space between my legs. I remember that bulb above me as my eyelids had been flickering in twisted pleasure. I heard the constant buzz of the bathroom fan and the softened sounds of the TV from the drawing-room. I saw the reflection of my contorted body on the shiny surface of that metal faucet, and I didn't like it. I closed my eyes, basking those uninterrupted and sloppy strokes of water on my clitoris. I did it repetitively. The stored water on the floor gradually lost the temperature to become lukewarm, then cold. I felt goosebumps pop up all over my body like I was wrapped in a bubble sheet."

"And what about your parents? Didn't they ever enquire about your obsession with spending so long in the bathroom?"

"No. They were typical middle-class parents who never bothered about anything except their daughter's marks in the exams. And I was a studious student, used to rank within the top ten students," she replied, playing with her large dolphin pendant, covered with innumerable tiny diamonds.

"I see! So basically, you became a loner due to your parents' aloofness, and that pushed you more towards that bad habit," Dr Khanna guessed.

"I don't think so. Though it's correct that my parents used to be busy in their struggle for existence and rarely had any time for me, but they were quite friendly with me. Papa was a marketing officer in a private company. He always had some or the other deadlines to meet, and Ba was a housewife who had given up her career for family."

"But Shanaya, being friendly can't compensate for their absence in your life. Anyway, let's continue your journey of exploration."

Shanaya nodded thoughtfully and continued, "Ayesha had invented a few more tricks which further enhanced our journey of pleasure even in public places. After finishing our group studies, we used to implement our mischievous ideas to customise our inner garments. Obviously, my home was the better place to stay behind the closed door for a longer period as compared to hers."

Shanaya giggled, covering her mouth and said, "It was so funny! We cut the elasticized straps from a few of our bras, got rid of all the hooks and other metal components, and sewed the end of one strap with another to make it lengthier. We used to keep that prolonged strap inside our panty, positioning it between our legs as one of its ends was fixed at our back with the elasticised waistband, letting the other end hang out of the panty for us to pull it from the top of our trouser, pyjama or even burqa. We named it 'clito-stroker'."

"So, you were happy with your self-gratification and never felt any need of other humans. Weren't you attracted to any man, emotionally or physically?"

"No, not at that age. I was a nerdy and introvert teenager who loved to read books staying at home most of the time rather than going out with friends. Moreover, I studied in a girls' school, having no chance of communication with any male classmates. Though a few guys in my neighbourhood had approached me, I didn't find any interest. After our tenth board exams, I lost touch with Ayesha. Her family married her off into another city.

"She always knew she would be forced to marry somebody she barely knew and didn't love. In her family, being a woman was all about being somebody else's property. She was like an object, expected to wait for men and produce children."

Shanaya became mute for a few moments as her eyes filled with mist. She looked outside the window hiding her tears and asked softly, "Don't you think we all are living with our own ghosts which are made up of our unfulfilled wishes and secret desires that are taboos to our society?"

"I understand you." Dr Khanna evaded her question.

She continued, "I have never earned any real friend with whom I can talk my heart out with, except Ayesha. Many people have stepped into my life as friends, but my acquaintance and conversations always remained formal. One day, Papa bought a computer, a desktop along with a dial-up internet connection. I downloaded a few online messengers and started talking to strangers. Gradually, my world shrank inside that nineteen-inch screen; those tiny black switches of the keyboard became my voice. My name, identity, and existence kept changing according to the perceptions of those strangers. I used to sit on the edge of my father's rotating, pushback chair, desperately waiting for the conversation prompt ASL, which means - age, sex, and location. Those chats predominantly followed with questions like, 'What are you wearing?', 'What's your bra size?' 'What's the colour of your nipples' and 'What do you want me to do to you?'."

Shanaya smiled blushing as she said, "And my answers used to be 'A lace thong, 36D, light brown and anything you want'. Obviously, I wasn't wearing a lace thong at home, and my tits were not even close to 36D, but none of that mattered. It was a world where you can take any size, shape or avatar, and words were the only weapon to win the heart and savour the pleasure. Eventually, I started ASLing others and became a part of that provocative virtual world. Along with random encounters, I also had some steady chat partners. Akhilesh, a thirty-two-year-old from Mumbai who liked fucking on his desk at work, mentioned the paperweight, stapler, pen, the keyboard, and other office stuffs to set the scene. Then, Aslam, a twenty-five-year-old from Hyderabad who described me fucking on elevators, in closets, and in other tight spaces. I started off submissively, replying in mere monosyllabic yes or no to any of their requests, and exposed only slight descriptors about my imaginary avatar. But gradually, I picked up words like 'cock' and 'blow job' and 'cum' and started knitting these things together. Later, I became an expert, describing myself so efficiently in words that any artist could paint me by just reading my chat history."

"Go on… I am all ears! Whatever you have told so far, is quite natural for a curious teenager," Dr Khanna encouraged.

"I had to leave my old school and took admission to another girl's school for my higher studies. A lot of new faces arrived in my life. However, I never wanted to meet any of them outside the school premises. My conversations with my new friends were restricted to some TV serials, nail-paint colours, shoes, and rarely some studies. Eventually, I became isolated and cybersex became my inevitable escapism from my bitter loneliness. In the long holidays during that summer, my habit of cybersex turned into my obsession. It impacted my studies badly. I used to look for opportunities to spend more time in that virtual world, and Ayesha's 'clito-stroker' became handy, continuing my journey of pleasure uninterruptedly, even when my parents were around. However, I started finding that process quite monotonous. Those repeating questions, answers and words weren't appealing to me anymore. Gradually, a morbid desire to taste real sex got the best of me, and my destiny provided me with an opportunity. During my summer vacation, Papa appointed a..."

Vayu paused the video as he picked up his mobile, receiving a call from Chaddha.

"Vayu, the doctor wants to brief on the autopsy report," Chaddha informed excitedly.

"I am coming."

Chaddha had been waiting for Vayu at the reception and guided him to the autopsy room. The arrival of Vayu and Chaddha interrupted the discussion between Abhimanyu and the doctor while all of them gathered around Shanaya's corpse, which was kept on a stretcher under a white sheet.

"I am not yet done with the formal post-mortem report; it will take a few more days. But I will brief you on my findings as I have been told that I am the bottleneck in your investigation. And my mobile has never stopped ringing for the last few days." The Doctor had more wrinkles on his face because of his irritation rather than his old age.

"I can understand," Abhimanyu empathised and continued, smirking after a glance at Vayu. "I am also going through the same pain. And this will increase in the future, if inefficient and inexperienced people start joining the department with bookish knowledge and illusions of crime-thriller movies."

Chaddha chuckled as he glanced at Vayu's face, hoping for his impassiveness to the provocation of Abhimanyu. Vayu remained indifferent to those conversations. He stood there, gazing at Shanaya's face. She wasn't just a corpse to him anymore after he had learnt the core of her mind. Medical examinations gave her many clean and lengthy stitches on her face. Vayu could hear her husky voice whispering in his ears in a lethargic way. The visions of her therapy sessions flashed in front of his eyes.

"Ricin is our killer." The doctor's loud voice pierced through Vayu's ears. He looked at the doctor blankly.

"What is Ricin?" Abhimanyu asked.

"It's a poison found naturally in castor beans. The major castor producing states in India are Gujarat, Rajasthan and Andhra Pradesh. These castor beans are processed to make castor oil and ricin is part of the waste mash produced when castor oil is made. It can be in the form of a powder, a mist or a pellet, or it can be dissolved in water or weak acid. In 1978, Georgi Markov, a Bulgarian writer and journalist, died after being attacked by a man with an umbrella. The umbrella had been rigged to inject a poison, ricin pellet under his skin. Some reports say that ricin has possibly been used as a warfare agent in the 1980s in Iraq and more recently by few terrorist organizations," Vayu said under one breath.

"Impressive!" the doctor appreciated.

"Sometimes, it's better to not wait for life to teach us everything. We can proactively learn in advance. And I believe, some documentaries, movies and old crime case studies are helpful in learning," Vayu said, looking at the doctor.

Chaddha chuckled again and Abhimanyu kept quiet.

"There is no doubt that Shanaya had inhaled the poison. But I am not sure whether she was exposed to it accidentally or someone else did it. I mean, whether it's an accident or a murder," Vayu murmured softly. Looking carefully at her face, he inquired, "Do you have any clue, doctor?"

"It's a murder. Ricin gets inside the cells of our body and prevents the cells from making the proteins they need. Eventually, cells die. I have found many cells in her body, which had died a few months back, approximately three months. It started from her nostrils and spread throughout her body," the doctor explained his conclusion.

"That means she had been exposed to poison for three months," Vayu said disappointedly and whispered after a few seconds of muteness, "That disrupts the complete timeline and suspect pool of our investigation. It takes us back to square one."

"Effects of ricin poisoning depend on whether ricin was inhaled, ingested or injected. Oral exposure to ricin is far less toxic as the poison might be inactivated in the stomach. Shanaya hasn't swallowed or chewed it. She has been inhaling that toxic substance in a negligible amount since the last few months before her death. Our killer planned it precisely, making her inhale a tiny amount of ricin frequently," the doctor elaborated.

"So, the killer must be a frequent visitor," Abhimanyu concluded.

"I don't think so. The choice of the murder weapon suggests that the killer wanted to keep a safer distance from Shanaya. The delayed death of the victim provided the killer ample time to wipe off all possible traces," Vayu commented thoughtfully.

"You are brilliant! You have left no blood, no wound, no murder weapon, no fingerprint, or any other trace on your prey to reach you, like a ghost. It has been killing the victim little by little every day in front of everyone. And you turned that delay in your favour like a sandstorm to hide your crime. I can't reach you without mere serendipity of circumstances," Vayu mused, staring at the cadaver.

"I see! Are you saying that the killer poisoned something she was habituated to use regularly?" Abhimanyu asked. Vayu nodded his affirmation.

The post-mortem report pushed Vayu to a critical conjuncture. Shanaya's casual flings had already increased the suspect pool to endless uncertainty. Moreover, the fact of slow poisoning had expanded the timeline to the extent that Vayu couldn't track. Tracking three months of a dead woman's life and retrieve that tiny moment when she had started inhaling that poison, was next to impossible. There were many doubts, uncertainties, puzzles, and questions that made Vayu so uncomfortable that he couldn't sleep that night. However, his tired eyelids gave up at the end, just before dawn.

He awakened to the sound of his mobile. Keeping his eyes closed, he fumbled for it on the bed.

"Hello," he mumbled in a sleepy voice.

"Good morning, sir! We have found Oorja's house. It would be great if you can have a first-hand view of the place," Dubey responded.

"Who is Oorja?" Vayu asked as he dragged himself on the bed to sit.

"That murder victim of Dive Inn. Remember that ghost I asked your suggestion to find the whereabouts of."

"Oh, yes. Okay, I am coming," Vayu muttered, massaging his temples and forehead to soothe the headache from sleep deprivation.

Vayu took note of the address on his mobile.

Yusuf pulled out a small knife from his bag and tucked it in the rear of his trouser belt. He wrapped a towel around his face and adjusted it to hide his face properly except the eyes, carefully observing his reflection in a puddle of water on the muddy floor. One of his acquaintances in Badshahpur had arranged a cowshed for their hideout in exchange for a hefty amount.

"Get up!" he called out, tapping on Suraj's shoulder. After a momentary interruption, Suraj resumed his snoring.

Yusuf kicked him in the hips and screamed, "*Bhosdike! Apne baap ki barat mein aaya hai kya?* Get your ass off from this haystack. It's not safe for us to stay in one place for a long time. We will be roaming around the nearby villages and towns till sunset."

Suraj spent a few moments in shock, lying there with his open eyes and a blank face before he responded, "*Bhai, mujhe ghar jana hai, apne biwi ke pass!*" He urged, rubbing his eyes, "I will listen to everything you say. But you will have to allow me to meet my wife at least once."

"For taking care of your wife, you should be alive first," Yusuf admonished, fetching a bunch of *bidis* from his pocket. He pulled out one *bidi* from the bunch, blew both the ends, and lit it.

"Why don't we surrender and tell all the truth to the police?" Suraj asked as he sat on the haystack, hugging his folded legs.

"*Koi movie chal rahi hai kya, bhenchod?* You will tell them the truth, and they will believe you. She is dead, it doesn't matter who…. *Tu woh sab chhod aur* ready *ho ja*," Yusuf snapped back, emitting the smoke from his nose and mouth.

"At least they won't kill us, right? We have the money, and that's not going anywhere. Think about it! We will get security of our lives," Suraj suggested as he stood up.

"But we don't know who all in the police department work for that gang. *Seedha* encounter *kar dega*. We can't risk," Yusuf replied, offering his *bidi* to Suraj. After a thoughtful silence,

Yusuf suggested, "Okay, I will let you go to meet your family. But you must start only after the sunset and return here before sunrise. Agree?"

Suraj nodded with a wide grin.

"The house is locked from the outside. Should we break the door?" Dubey asked as soon as Vayu reached Oorja's house.

"I am here to help you, Dubey *ji*. Not to take any decisions. I don't want to give Abhimanyu another excuse to blame and insult me. I think you should have sought his help first," Vayu said softly, putting on his sunglass as the scorching sunlight worsened his headache.

Dubey sighed, moved close to Vayu, and whispered, "He is not much interested in this case."

Vayu shrugged as Dubey asked one of the policemen in his small troop of five to break open the main entrance. The house was surrounded by abandoned plots, so they could break the door without attracting much attention. They spread all over the house and started combing each corner. Vayu and Dubey entered one of the two rooms at opposite sides of the hallway, along with two other policemen. Vayu noticed a discoloured patch on the wall, peeping from behind a slightly tilted portrait of a couple. Obviously, the metal frame of that picture had scratched out the plaster of that portion of the wall. Vayu reached close to that wall and adjusted the frame evenly aligning it. The patch on the wall wasn't visible anymore.

"*Kuchh nahi mila,* sir! There's nothing," one of the policemen informed Dubey.

"Would you like us to search in any particular portion?" Dubey asked Vayu.

Vayu shook his head and proposed, "Let's move to the other room."

Two of the policemen had already ransacked the other room, and one of them reported finding nothing suspicious while Vayu and Dubey arrived there.

"Dubey *ji*, I think we are late. Someone has been here before us," Vayu remarked, walking towards the cupboard.

He sat on his haunches near the bottom of the cupboard and said, "Look at these dragging marks on the floor. Someone has surely moved the closet."

He wiped that marked portion of the floor with his hand, and it became faint. He whispered to himself, "It's fresh."

He rose up and asked, "Dubey *ji*, do you remember the last time you rearranged or moved the heavy furniture of your home?"

"Yes, last Diwali."

"Exactly! The inhabitants of a house do this kind of work only during the festive season. But that is not the case here; no new painting on the wall, even the open portions of the floor are dusty, so is the closet itself," Vayu explained his theory. "There must be something behind the closet. Check that out!" Vayu ordered.

Four policemen had to put immense effort in moving that huge cupboard away from the wall, and they all could see a secret shelf on the wall. And it was empty, just as Vayu had expected.

"What's next? What do you suggest?" Dubey asked as all of them came out of Oorja's house and gathered on that muddy alley.

"Dubey *ji*, as I told you, this is something big. We must depend on…" Vayu hadn't finished his words as a dusky, tall and wide man in white vest and lungi distracted him. Vayu had noticed him at the other side of the alley when they were entering Oorja's house.

He rushed to that over-curious man and asked, "What's your name?"

"Gopal, sir."

"Have you seen anything suspicious around this house?" Vayu enquired.

Gopal nodded half-heartedly. It wasn't quite difficult for Vayu to read his mind. Vayu reached his back pocket, took out his purse, drew a note of five hundred rupees from it and held it in front of Gopal.

"This is just an advance. Isn't it, Dubey *ji*?" Vayu provoked.

Dubey nodded his affirmation to grab that remote opportunity which might help him to crack the murder.

"A few days back, I saw a man who had been trying to open the lock. *Ekdum hero mafik tha wo*... tall, fair and handsome. *Pehle kabhi nahi dekha usko is* area *mein*," Gopal informed with a lot of facial expressions and gesture to emphasise his words, hoping for a higher bid.

"Exactly how many days back?" Dubey asked impatiently.

"Three, no, two days back," Gopal fumbled and continued, "He had no idea about the correct key and kept trying one after another. That made me curious."

"That's the next day of the murder. That night I had called you for help," Dubey clarified as Vayu looked at him, raising a speculative eyebrow.

"He had a bandage on his head and one on his forearm," Gopal finished.

Vayu and Dubey exchanged glances as that description shook them to the core. It might be the man both were thinking about, or a mere coincidence.

"Can you come with us and describe his face in detail to our sketch artist?" Vayu asked. Dubey stood there in shock.

Gopal nodded in agreement and said, "But I need more money for that."

"That's absolutely fine," Vayu assured.

They started for the police station along with Gopal. On the way, Dubey called one of his men in the station and asked to arrange for a sketch artist. However, when they reached, Dubey learnt about the unavailability of any artist at that short notice. Compelled by the situation, they had to postpone the sketching until the next day. Dubey asked Gopal to revisit the next day and assured his reward.

Gopal walked out of the police station with a wide smile. He was so pleased with the mention of reward that he didn't notice Abhimanyu. However, Abhimanyu noticed and identified him immediately. He hurriedly pulled out a handkerchief from his pocket and covered his face. He hung out there for a few minutes letting Gopal reach the main street and followed him, maintaining a safe distance. Gopal boarded a bus and Abhimanyu hired an auto, ordering the driver to follow the bus. Gopal got off the bus at a stop near Oorja's house, crossed the road and walked towards that same blind alley that passed by her house. Gopal entered the alley, reached the dead-end of it, and knocked on the door of a small house on the right. A little girl opened the door with a pleasing smile and spread out her arms. Gopal picked up the little girl, hugged her, and vanished inside the house. Abhimanyu kept stalking him from a little far and rushed towards the dead-end immediately after Gopal entered his home. Abhimanyu had a good look at the door wall, and overall appearance of that house and reached back to the main road.

Abhimanyu reached Dubey's desk as soon as he returned to office and enquired, "Is there any progress on that Drive Inn murder case?"

Dubey sprung up, leaving his chair and answered, "Yes, sir. We have identified the victim and found her local residence as well." That was the first time Dubey had a gloominess on his face and a discomforting voice while reporting a huge breakthrough in a murder case.

"Wow! That's awesome, Dubey *ji*," Abhimanyu appreciated with a smile and asked, "Have you searched the house?"

"Yes, but we did not find any lead over there." Dubey had a smile of relief on his face and confidence in his voice, though he was talking about failure. Abhimanyu's false happiness on the progress of investigation made Dubey believe that Abhimanyu was innocent. Dubey felt an immense comfort as he continued, "But we have found a witness Gopal who saw a man breaking into her house. He will come and describe that man to our sketch artist tomorrow. That man surely has some connection with Oorja's murder."

"Hmm... Good job, Dubey ji. That's commendable," Abhimanyu praised, patting him on his shoulder.

"Vayu sir helped me a lot. Otherwise it wouldn't have been possible in such a short time."

Abhimanyu nodded, raising his eyebrows, and left for his cabin. On the way, he asked Chaddha to see him in his cabin, along with Vayu.

Chaddha found Vayu at his desk, leaning on the table, hiding his face with folded arms by the laptop. It was an unusual sight for Chaddha.

"Vayu, what happened? Are you alright?" he asked, gently placing his hand on his shoulder.

Vayu raised himself up from the table on one elbow, adjusted himself on the chair to sit straight, and asked with a brief yawn, "Yes, I am fine. Just a little sleep-deprived."

"Abhimanyu has asked us to meet him in his cabin."

"Let's go!"

"Please try to avoid him if he provokes you for any kind of argument, just a request," Chaddha added. Vayu nodded, standing up on his feet.

"So, whom are we arresting today?" Abhimanyu asked as they stepped into his room. He didn't even ask them to sit.

"I don't think we are in a position to arrest anyone," Vayu retorted, pulling a chair for himself. Chaddha kept standing by Vayu.

"And why so? Weren't we just waiting for the autopsy report?" Abhimanyu asked, smirking.

"Yes, but that report couldn't help us much. Moreover...."

Abhimanyu raised his palm, gesturing Vayu to become silent, leaned on the table in front of him, and said, "We need an arrest within the next forty-eight hours. Department is under tremendous pressure from the government. Solve your own case before helping others. Haven't you heard that instruction on the flight? Help yourself before helping others."

There was pin-drop silence in the room until Abhimanyu ordered, "You may leave now, and keep me posted."

Vayu had a dreadful stillness on his face as he zoned out, his eyes pinned to a doll hanging from the rear view mirror. Chaddha stole a few glances in between his driving, but didn't try to make any conversation with him. Chaddha chuckled as he thought that Abhimanyu shouldn't have talked like that. According to him, in that period of crisis, they all should work as a team. He closed his eyes and prayed for a breakthrough at Shanaya's mansion.

"Suspicion always haunts the guilty mind; The thief doth fear each bush an officer," Vayu muttered with a smile on his face.

"Haan ji?" Chaddha asked in surprise.

"Nothing! A quote by William Shakespeare."

"Do you think Abhimanyu can murder someone or protect a killer?" Vayu asked.

Chaddha became mute for a moment before saying, "See, I know, he shouldn't have insulted you like that. But he is not that bad, you know. It's just his depressed mind and that shit he consumes all the time."

"No, Chaddha *ji*, something big is going on in front of our eyes, and we cannot see it." Vayu had wrinkles of uncertainty on his face. After a few quiet moments, Vayu asked, "Why is my involvement in the Drive Inn murder case disturbing Abhimanyu?"

"Because he wants you to conclude Shanaya's murder case first. You know that the department is under huge pressure."

The Sinful Silence • 137

"I don't think so. I can smell something fishy. Anyway, there won't be any cloud of suspicion tomorrow after we get the sketch," Vayu stated firmly. Chaddha nodded, supporting his belief.

Chaddha parked the vehicle at the same spot as on his previous visit to Shanaya's mansion. The security guard identified them and invited Chaddha and Vayu inside. He guided them to that same living room decorated with many large portraits of Shanaya and her family, requested them to wait there and hurried upstairs.

After a couple of minutes, Shanaya's husband Manoj came down the stairs along with an old man in a white shirt, trousers and black coat and gestured them to wait a little more with an apologetic expression. He walked the old man to the iron gate as he discussed something in a low voice and returned to the living room after bidding him goodbye.

"Wow! So, the party has begun?" Vayu taunted Manoj as he settled on the couch opposite them.

Manoj opened his mouth to say something, but Vayu continued in denial to hear him, "The corpse of your wife has been waiting for justice in the morgue and you have started warming your inherited eggs from your wife. She might have left huge wealth for you. Isn't it, Mr Sharma? Despite being a piece of shit, she loved you the most."

Chaddha looked at Vayu in shock and whispered, "Vayu, that's not our business." He had never seen such an unprofessional, emotional and child-like behaviour from Vayu before, and he blamed Abhimanyu in his mind for that situation.

"You don't know shit about our relationship. So don't even try to judge me," Manoj shrieked as he got up from the couch, losing his temper. He walked away from them a few steps aimlessly, turned back, and shouted, "Yes, I was a piece of shit for her. Just a piece of shit to secure her decent marital status to the society and hide her real character of a whore. You cannot even imagine how I felt when she used to go out in the middle of the night, putting makeup on her face, all dressed up to seduce other men? Yes, I summoned a lawyer to have a better understanding of my wage for tolerating a whore for fifteen years."

"I don't expect a person like you to understand her anyway. But it reflects your stupidity, that you took fifteen years to convince your wife for her property and murder her," Vayu snapped back.

Manoj screamed, "How dare you to accuse me without any proof? I know you guys quite well. When you fail in cracking any case, you just arrest an innocent person to hide your failure. Bloody losers!"

"We are here to search this whole property. Please cooperate with us," Chaddha jumped in, putting an end to the word fight.

"Show me the search warrant," Manoj demanded.

Chaddha sighed, taking a glimpse of Vayu's face as his imprudent act had made their smooth job difficult.

"We don't need a search warrant as this is the house of the victim herself. And don't try to act smart. That will only make it easy for me to put your ass behind bars," Vayu warned, pouring out all his anger and frustration for Abhimanyu on Manoj.

Manoj plunged himself back on the couch like an arrogant kid and gestured at them to start their search.

"Vayu, first of all, we couldn't arrange for any search team in such a short time," Chaddha told in a low voice while they started climbing the stairs. Vayu nodded as he hopped across a couple of stairs.

"We two are not enough to search this huge bungalow," Chaddha told, huffing as he pulled himself, grabbing the wooden railing of the staircase to match Vayu's speed. Vayu nodded, reaching upstairs.

Three bedrooms on the first floor were connected by a long and narrow carpeted corridor. Vayu entered one of those bedrooms, which was nearest from the landing of the staircase. Chaddha followed him limping, but before he could enter the room, Vayu came out of it and started walking towards the next room.

"Moreover, we...we don't know what we are looking for!" Chaddha fumbled from behind as he bent over, holding his knees.

"We could have asked Manoj to guide us through this giant property. But you have wasted that thin chance," Chaddha said panting while Vayu turned back and waited for him to join. Chaddha raised himself and limped towards Vayu.

"See, it's simple. We are looking for something which emits poison that took three months to kill Shanaya. It must be something that she was habituated to inhale regularly. So, obviously, it must be placed somewhere where Shanaya used to spend most of her time during her stay at home. Now, she seldom used to spend time at home due to her busy business schedules, except nights. So, we should start our search in the bedroom. If what we are looking for is present in this mansion, it must be in her bedroom," Vayu explained as he had a glimpse of all the bedrooms tagging along with Chaddha.

"Let's start from this room. This must be hers," Vayu said, pointing at the biggest bedroom among those three.

"Have a look at your tummy, Chaddha *ji*. Breakfast *mein rava dosa khaya kijiye. Aloo paratha* health *ke lie achchha nahi hai.* Otherwise, join Rizwan's gym," Vayu advised as he entered the bedroom. Chaddha reluctantly stepped into the room following Vayu.

Chaddha chuckled and said, "I have only a few months left to retire."

It wouldn't be wrong to call it a great hall rather than a bedroom. There was a king-size bed in the middle of that room. A large mirror, two couches, a centre table, a couple of bedside tables, night lamps, and a modern chandelier dangling over the bed, everything had a soothing grey and silver colour to create a sparkling, luxurious feel. The plush silvery grey carpet practically begged for their bare feet. Waking up in this bedroom would be like waking up inside a warm storm cloud. One of the four walls of that room was made of a sliding glass and the door opened to a balcony.

"That might be the bathroom, let's start from there," Vayu suggested, pointing at the closed door.

They entered the bathroom to find a large Jacuzzi, a ceramic one-piece pedestal washbasin, a ceramic wall hanging commode, and a tall mirror with a closet. Everything was white in colour, matching with the marble walls.

Vayu walked closer to the Jacuzzi, kneeled on the floor near its headrest, bent over it, and ordered, "Get me the gloves."

He picked up a few broken pieces of a candle wearing the gloves and said, "Chaddha *ji*, keep it in a pouch. We should keep each of these objects in different pouches."

Chaddha nodded. Vayu opened the closet and collected the few perfume bottles, a packet of incense, and a bottle of air-freshener in separate pouches.

"Don't know how many days we have to wait again for the report of these things," Vayu murmured in frustration as they come out of the bathroom. Chaddha made a puppy face to indicate that he had no clue.

"What's that?" Vayu pointed at a pitcher-shaped device on the left bedside table.

"Must be a night lamp," Chaddha said as they reached close to it.

It had two distinguishable parts – a blue transparent upper part with a few millilitres of water in it and a solid white lower part with three switches and a latch.

"Nope, it's a humidifier," Vayu said after observing it minutely. He slid the latch, separated the transparent portion from the device, and said, "Have you seen this stored water?"

Chaddha nodded like a curious kid, leaned on that a little more, and asked, "*Pani garam karta hai kya?*"

"No, it emits water vapours or steam to increase the moisture levels in the air. In addition to that, some people use it as an air freshener as well," Vayu informed as he pulled the drawer of that bedside table to find a book and a few files.

"There should be some bottles of essential oils somewhere," he murmured as he tugged the second drawer in a hurry.

A pleasant smile waved on his face to see those tiny bottles of essential oils. They were labelled with white stickers with handwritten names on them.

"Collect them, Chaddha *ji*!" Vayu's voice trembled in excitement as he told, "I think we have found the murder weapon."

Chaddha sat on the edge of the bed and started collecting each of the bottles in separate pouches.

"Do you remember that aroma in Dr Khanna's office?" Vayu asked as he picked up one of those bottles form the drawer and read the label on it, 'lemongrass + tea tree'.

"Nope, I just remember that couch. *Ekdum mast tha!*" Chaddha replied, laughing, and kept his hands busy in collecting those bottles of essential oils.

"It was a mix of lemongrass and lavender. Shanaya didn't buy these oils directly from any shop. These handwritten labels are proof of that. And I believe it's Dr Khanna who gave these bottles to Shanaya to use for stress relief and sound sleep," Vayu muttered thoughtfully, handing over the bottle in his hand to Chaddha.

"I knew it. I told you that doctor is the culprit!" Chaddha shrieked in a thrill.

"But what could be his motive, and moreover, we are not sure about the presence of any poison in these essential oils. But we can move ahead with our assumption that these bottles contain ricin. I strongly believe that the lab report will support us later," Vayu completed.

"Obviously, property. Dr Khanna might have managed to convince Shanaya to give him some portion or the entire property."

"Possible. There is another possibility... that Manoj and Khanna have teamed up and poisoned Shanaya based on a deal of sharing the property. Manoj must have a big portion of Shanaya's property in his name, and he needed it immediately to pay those usurers. After learning about her flings, another reason got added to kill her, which is revenge," Vayu explained in a low voice as they came out of the bedroom.

"In that case, we can't ask Manoj about the source of these oils." Chaddha said, walking through the corridor along with Vayu.

"But, these two assumptions are self-contradictory. If these oils contain ricin, then Manoj is not the murderer," Vayu said. He further explained after a pause of reading the clueless and blank expression of Chaddha, "Manoj had ample time to hide these oils after Shanaya's death, but he didn't do it. It implies, either he is the unsub, or these oils are not his murder weapon. And if the lab-report shows the presence ricin in these oils and they have come from Dr Khanna, then we just need to find the final missing piece that Shanaya had willed some property to Dr Khanna."

"No problem in that. I will find Shanaya's lawyer and confirm it," Chaddha assured as they started descending the staircase.

While they returned to the drawing-room on the ground floor, Manoj pretended to be busy reading the newspaper after stealing a glance. Vayu walk past him without a word and got out of the mansion. Chaddha bid him a formal goodbye and joined Vayu outside. Chaddha kept all the pouches safely in the glove compartment of their SUV, settled himself on the driving seat, fastened the seat belt and waited for Vayu to get in.

"Did you see that woman who served us tea on our last visit?" Vayu asked.

Chaddha shook his head and asked, "What about her?"

"She should know about these small things in Shanaya's room. After all, that's her job, housekeeping. Isn't it?" His voice was soft as he mused to himself and rushed to the security guard before Chaddha could react.

"Do you know about that woman who works here?" Vayu asked the security guard.

"Yes sir, Manju. But she has not been coming to work for the last three days."

"Do you know her address?"

The security guard told them the address. Vayu repeated it a few times in his mind, rushed back to the SUV and said in excitement, "Chaddha *ji*, let's go! I think my hunch is correct."

Abhimanyu took a lengthy puff at his cigarette as he plunged himself in knitting a plan which could assure self-preservation. There was a riot of thoughts in his mind like the wisps of silver-grey smoke curling and dancing their way through his nostrils. Should he clog Gopal's mouth with a hefty sum? No, no. That would portray the punier side of him, which might encourage him to blackmail him in the future. He didn't want to create another Mukund. Should he scare the shit out of him? What if he would decide to take a risk for money! After all, Abhimanyu wasn't aware of how desperate he was. And killing him was certainly not a wise decision at that moment.

"There is no other way, but one," Abhimanyu murmured to himself, choosing the option that he hated the most. Life had taught him that every devil had a little bird where he hid his life. The devil might not care about his own life, but always for the little bird's.

He received the call pulling out his mobile from the pocket as it rang and smirked, glancing at the number.

"Yes," he responded.

"Sir, it's Mukund, your biggest fan. I know you still have a few more days. It's just a gentle reminder. After all, you are a busy person."

The call got disconnected. Abhimanyu threw the cigarette butt on the ground and smashed it under his feet.

Chaddha drove following Vayu's direction and reached an area in sector 5, which was occupied by many shanties.

He parked the vehicle by the main road and said, "It won't be easy to find Manju in this huge slum."

"We have no other option, sir," Vayu said, comprehending the reluctance in Chaddha's voice.

They got off the vehicle and entered the slum. It had several narrow and dingy lanes which spread through the congested shanties. The houses were nothing but single room tenements without the facilities of an open courtyard or an enclosure, thus depriving the people of natural gifts like sunshine and air. Few of those shanties were just thick clusters of small, dilapidated mud huts, the roofs and ceilings made of scraps of wood, gunny sacks, metal or some sort of waste material. The stagnant sewage water in the open surface drains had been overflowing in many places and made those narrow lanes an integral part of the drainage. Chaddha reached into his right-hand pocket, pulled out a handkerchief and covered his nose and mouth.

Vayu smiled softly, noticing him and said, "Chaddha *ji*, you should have used your hanky in Shanaya's bedroom. I wonder whether we have inhaled some poison already. This is just foul smell, not poison."

"Sorry Vayu, I can't talk right now." Chaddha managed to answer him in a hushed-up voice covering his mouth and nose.

They started asking random people on their way whether they know anyone named Manju. And it took them almost thirty-five minutes to reach her home. Her shanty was bigger and better in comparison to others. A scrawny old woman in white saree and blouse opened the door as Chaddha knocked the small and partly decayed wooden door. She was holding the door for support . She kept staring at them with a blank expression.

"*Maa ji, Manju ghar pe hai?*" Chaddha asked screaming, presuming the old woman to be hard of hearing.

"*Chilla kyu rahe ho? Wo ghar pe nahi hai*, hospital *mein hai*," the old woman answered in anger.

"*Hua kya?*" Chaddha asked softly this time.

"*Pata nahi, kuch tabiyat kharab thi*. Bhimrao Ambedkar hospital *mein bharti hui hai*."

They rushed to Dr Bhimrao Ambedkar Multi-speciality Hospital in sector 30. Vayu hurried towards the entrance.

Vayu rushed to the enquiry desk and asked the man, "I need some information about a patient named Manju."

"Sir, may I know your relationship with the patient?" the man enquired.

Vayu had to flash his badge in the absence of his uniform.

"Okay! Do you know her last name or address?" that man asked.

"Not sure about the last name but resides in that slum area of sector 5," Vayu replied.

That man nodded and started checking his computer for any match with that minimal information. In the meanwhile, Chaddha reached there, huffing.

"Yes, sir. Please go to…"

Before he could finish his sentence, Vayu interrupted, "I want to meet the doctor who has been treating her."

"Dr Deepak Mohanty; second last room on the right side of this corridor."

Vayu started walking towards the directed room, Chaddha tagging behind.

"May I come in, sir?" Vayu asked for permission.

They entered, hearing a male voice that said "Please" from inside.

The middle-aged man with average build, Dr Deepak Mohanty was startled by their unexpected arrival as Chaddha's uniform had given him an unspoken introduction about them.

"How...how, may I help you?" he fumbled to ask and gestured at them to have a seat.

"It's okay, we won't take much of your time; just a quick question. What exactly happened to your patient Manju?" Vayu asked.

Dr Mohanty kept staring at them for seconds in confusion and said, "See, I have so many patients I visit every day. So, I can't remember each and everyone's names. I must check the records. Please have a seat."

"That guy at your enquiry desk referred us to you when we asked about Manju. You might take his help to find her quickly," Vayu suggested, occupying a chair. Chaddha sat on another chair by him.

Dr Mohanty nodded in unanimity, called that person at the enquiry desk, and asked him to bring Manju's medical file. That man arrived in five minutes with the file. Dr Mohanty riffled through every page of that file before keeping it aside.

"It looks like she has been exposed to some kind of poison."

"I knew it!" Vayu screamed, banging the table.

Dr Mohanty was quite shocked by such boisterous behaviour. Chaddha asked Vayu to relax. Dr Mohanty looked at him for an explanation.

"Is it ricin?" Vayu asked.

The doctor nodded in affirmation reluctantly, expecting another bang on his table.

However, Vayu thanked him with a grinning face and asked, "Can we meet the patient?"

"Yes, of course! She is completely out of danger now." The doctor said as he stood up from his chair. "Please! Come with me."

"We are keeping her just for some routine observations. And she will be released tomorrow if everything is normal," Dr Mohanty informed on the way towards the ward where Manju had been allotted a bed.

Manju looked quite devastated in her blue hospital gown and messy hair. She dragged herself on the bed in a hurry to sit as they reached there.

"Relax...relax!" Vayu said politely.

Chaddha's uniform made other patients, nurses and hospital staff quite curious about their arrival. Some of them gathered around Manju's bed. Vayu looked at Dr Mohanty.

"Back to work, right now!" Dr Mohanty ordered loudly, comprehending Vayu's unspoken words.

"Hello Manju, are you feeling good now?" Vayu asked as that gathering broke off.

Manju started crying, not answering Vayu. Tears overflowed from her eyes, rolled over her dusky cheeks. Chaddha was about to tell her to stop crying and answer Vayu's question. However, Vayu showed his hand to refrain him from interfering. That was really the first person Vayu was witnessing who cried over Shanaya's death. And certainly, Shanaya hadn't willed anything in Manju's name. Real love and care are always selfless, Vayu thought.

"*Han sahab. Achchhe logon ke sath achchha kyun nahi hota,*" Manju murmured weeping over bad things happening to good people.

"You must have noticed a humidifier in her bedroom. Any idea where those bottles of essential oils came from?" Vayu asked softly, leaning close to the bed.

Manju looked baffled as she took a glimpse of everyone's faces.

"*Woh ek* machine *hai na teri* madam *ke* bedroom *mein, jis mein se khusboodar dhuan nikalta hai,*" Chaddha explained in Hindi.

"*Han... han,*" Manju said, nodding.

"*Uske andar jo* scent *dalta hai na, who kahan se ata tha?*" Chaddha asked further.

"Shanaya madam *ki dawai*. Doctor sahab *ne diya tha achchhi neend ke lie*." There was a glow in her eyes while she was talking, a proud feeling for her contribution to helping police catch the killer of her beloved madam.

"Do you know the name of the doctor?" Vayu asked.

"Name..." Manju muttered reminiscing. She gazed at the ceiling for moments before shouting the name, "Rahul!" Vayu and Chaddha exchanged a glance and smiled.

Vayu thanked Dr Mohanty and Manju for their cooperation before leaving.

"So, we just need the lab report to prove the presence of rice in those oils?" Chaddha asked as they approached the parking area.

"It's ricin, Chaddha *ji*. And more than the lab report, we need to know whether Shanaya had willed any property to Dr Khanna. A motive is the most precious finding in any investigation. It's a motive that drives us to do anything in our lives. We don't even fart without a motive."

Chaddha nodded like an obedient student.

Vayu was sure the next day would turn out to be big for him. Chaddha had already sent those essential oils for forensic tests and convinced the pathologist to conclude the test within the next twelve hours. Vayu had respect for Chaddha for that very reason. He had that quality to become indispensable until one falls into unanimity with him. Moreover, the availability of the sketch-artist would get Dubey a significant lead in his investigation of Oorja's murder case.

Vayu was well-acquainted with the fact that the anxiety and thrill in his mind wouldn't allow him to sleep that night. Hence, he started watching Shanaya's therapy session.

"During my summer vacation, Papa appointed a carpenter to make a new closet, a few chairs and repairing some old and damaged furniture. There was a free space in our dining hall just by the table that he changed into his workspace. Unintentionally, I developed a habit of stalking him. The first day he came with his father, and he was looking so reluctant to do that job. It seemed like he had been pressurised to be in his father's shoes and become a carpenter; his eyes had some other dream. Eventually, my hunch turned out to be a fact, he was a woodcrafter rather than a carpenter. He created many tiny dolls, statues and abstract wood arts with those unusable wood blocks. He used to tie his shoulder-length hair in a bun and take off his shirt before starting his work. Those holes in his white vest seemed quite fashionable to me, though they were just worn out spots. Alex had a tattoo on his neck, just below his bun, a couple of fiery wings.

"Who is Alex?" Dr Khanna asked.

"Oh! Sorry, I forgot to mention; his name was Alex. He was an artistic soul, shackled by a heavy burden of reality and quite attractive to awaken my senses and desires; lean, tall and fair. I loved to watch him working all day long, his wooden dust-covered strong forearms and popped up veins on them, and how he used to blow his hair out of his face in that weirdly endearing way."

Shanaya giggled, playing with the dolphin hanging from her necklace, lost in her nostalgia trip.

"I am sorry! I think you don't need this kind of detail. Am I right?" She asked after a few seconds of silence when she got hold of her attention in the present.

"It's not about what I need to hear. It's all about what you want to tell me," Dr Khanna said.

Shanaya nodded, flipping her lips.

"I am trying to find that trigger point of your life, that actually changed you. No one can tell me what it was, other than you. I am just here to ask you few specific questions to set the path, which will eventually lead you to that trigger point."

Vayu heard Dr Khanna's theatrical voice. He paused the video and went to look for some midnight snacks.

It was 11.30 p.m. when Suraj reached the highway. He had covered his face completely, except the eyes, obeying Yusuf's admonition. As Yusuf had warned him to not board any kind of public transport, he started waving at all the trucks. Many trucks passed by, before a jumbo truck loaded with vegetables halted in front of him.

The driver hung his head out of the window and shouted, "*Kidhar jana hai?*"

"Jasana," Suraj shouted to defeat the noise of the engine.

The driver gestured him to hop on the cargo bed of the truck. The driver started as Suraj whistled after getting on the truck.

Vayu resumed the video as he returned with some peanuts and chakli.

"One day, Ba went out to attend a social function in our neighbourhood, leaving us alone. I couldn't afford to miss that opportunity and broke the ice," Shanaya said with a mischievous hint of a smile on her lips.

She giggled for a moment and said, "He didn't notice that I was standing by him as his whole concentration was on measuring those woodblocks. I still remember his startled gaze while picking up one of his crafted wooden dolls and appreciating his art. He felt shy, took a glimpse of my face, and smiled nervously. I didn't speak a word. I asked him, 'Would you teach me wood crafting?' He kept measuring and marking those woodblocks with a pencil, ignoring my question.

"After a few minutes, he tucked the pencil behind his ear and looked at me. He had a light brown dreamy pair of eyes. 'It's a waste of time, madam,' he replied in his heavy voice. 'Then why do you do it?' I asked him. 'This art motivates me to live my life. It's food for my soul,' he replied, evading his eyes from meeting mine. After a silence, he smirked and said, "But it can't get me food for my stomach. Please don't complain to my father that I do all these during my working hours. He will kill me," Not only his facial expression, but his whole body had also been evincing the pain of his broken dream.

"I don't know why I said, 'I will tell your father if you don't teach me. And I will pay you the tuition fees.' He smiled innocently, and all I could think was, 'Oh, shit! What's going on inside me.' He was not particularly special looking. However, I was attracted to his soft, pure and artistic personality with the kind of heady trance that brings a butterfly to nectar. We started spending more time together with an excuse for learning wood crafting. My parents had no objection to that. Gradually, we started sharing many slices of our lives as we were getting comfortable with each other. I don't know whether it was love, but I had been basking his presence around me.

"Eventually, another day arrived when we were left alone at home. He wanted to teach me pyrography that day."

"What is pyrography?" Dr Khanna asked.

"Pyrography is the art of burning wood or leather to write or draw something. It literally means the act of writing with fire. He taught me how to use the wood burner tool. It was like a pen with a heated metallic tip to burn the surface of the wood. He had a lot of different sizes of tips to draw different shapes.

"My hand shook severely as the tip of the wood-burner touched the wooden surface for the first time. It burnt that portion emitting smoke and made a big hole. He knelt on the floor behind me, held my hand from behind, and whispered close to my ear, 'Relax!'"

He squeezed my fist, which held the burner and said, "Loosen up your grip on the pen so that you can move the burner freely."

I felt his warm breathing on my bare neck. It pushed me to the edge of my self-possession. I loosened up my grip and made a deep burning mark on that wooden surface.

He rubbed his thumb softly on my forearm like a feather and whispered, "Don't scratch the wood so deep, rub it tenderly like this. Try to..."

I couldn't control myself anymore. I turned back and cut him off by kissing his lips. That startled him. I thought he didn't like it and it might be the last time we saw each other. I was scared to lose him forever. We both gazed into each other's eyes longingly, not a word spoken by either of us. My gaze slid to the side. He pulled me against his chest. His nose tickled my ear. And soon, he clutched my hips, leaning me in against his body. I was weakened by his gentle, seductive touch. The burner fell on the floor from my grasp as I held his forearms impulsively and tried to push them away. He kept gazing into my eyes while pressing his body against mine and begun kissing my frail neck which made me even weaker than before. I know it was wrong, but I wanted it so bad. The devil's cruel intention was already a success. There was only one desire in my mind, and my mind was prepared for the fact that it was just a matter of time before it happened.

"But my body wasn't habituated of those touches. He knew that once he kissed my neck, my resistance would smash. After just a few delicate touches of his warm lips on my lips, chin, throat and chest, my hands started doing his bidding. My breathing hastened, the intense rhythm of my heartbeat messed up, hammering quicker than the lightning bolt, as his hand slithered on my body, searching for the zip of my dress. My frock fell on the floor soon after. He could easily unhook my bra, but he took his pleasure of caressing my bare back and reaching it. Instead of opening the hook, his hands instantly flipped me over violently. He buried his head into my neck, and his hands roved all over my body. Our breathing became rough and fast. He grabbed the middle of the bra and yanked. I heard the fabric rip, and he grabbed my breasts from behind. He took all of me and savoured every moment of it. So did I."

Shanaya picked up the glass water which was placed on the table in front of her, sipped the water, placed the glass back on the table, and said, "That's the story of me losing my virginity."

"And that's completely normal, according to me. I didn't find any trigger points there. We will continue the search in our next session," Dr Khanna concluded.

The screen became blank. Vayu switched off the TV and went to catch some sleep.

Suraj had a permanent smile on his face as he boarded another truck for returning to Badshahpur after visiting his family. He had given his pregnant wife and parents enough money to live their lives comfortably during his absence. He hung his head out of the window and savoured the chilled wind of early morning on his face. He was lucky to get a seat inside the cabin of the truck. He was tired enough to doze off soon.

He awoke to the patting of the driver as the truck reached Badshahpur. He tipped the driver for his favour and started walking towards their hideout. The sky softened to a blue and the clouds blushed like a ripe mango. He started walking faster, remembering Yusuf's firm rebuke for failing to reach the cowshed before sunrise, and finally, he started running.

Suraj noticed a gathering in front of that cowshed from a distance. He stopped running further and started walking stealthily. He could feel his heart thumping on his ribcage as he walked closer to the gathering. Behind all the heads of those gathered villagers, he could see the hustle of a few khaki uniforms. For a split second, he decided to run away from there. But morbid curiosity got the best of him and he walked further. He peeped from behind a few people to find Yusuf's dead body. The corpse was lying on the ground in a puddle of blood with his throat slit. Suraj held the cloth with which he covered his face with, to his mouth as a wave of nausea clutched his stomach. He made his way out of that crowd. He refrained from running, held his nerve, and started walking towards the highway, not attracting anyone's attention.

"What about Shanaya's attorney?" Vayu asked Chaddha while they were waiting for the lab report in the hospital corridor.

"I tried reaching out, but he was out for some work. I managed to get his mobile number from his secretary," Chaddha said, reaching into his trousers' pocket and fetched out his mobile. He searched the number in his contact list and handed over his mobile to Vayu.

"Sunil Jha," Vayu muttered as he saved the number in his mobile.

Meanwhile, the expert arrived there and said without wasting any time, "I have found the presence of ricin in those essential oils; all of them are poisoned."

Vayu and Chaddha exchanged a glance of relief.

"However, I can't publish the report today. There are several formalities to be taken care of before that. However, my statement about the report is official, and you can refer it in your investigation," the doctor added.

"I am grateful for your favour, doctor!" Vayu expressed his gratitude.

"I am not the bottleneck in your investigation anymore," the doctor concluded and went inside his lab.

Vayu called Sunil Jha's number while they approached the hospital's parking, but didn't get any response.

"Okay, I will try again on the way to the station. Let's go, Chaddha ji! The sketch artist might have arrived already." Vayu was excited and thriller while Chaddha switched on the ignition.

"*Ek dum hero jaisa dikhne mein tha wo*; sharp nose, defined jaw line, fair, tall and handsome. I can identify him even in a crowded place. He had a bandage on his head and stubble on his face. And yes…"

"Wait…wait! Just describe the face in detail; not so vaguely," the sketch artist interrupted Gopal and instructed, "Let's start with the shape of his face, okay?"

The Sinful Silence • 157

"Square," Gopal answered monosyllabically.

"Skinny right; I mean no extra fat on the cheeks, jaws or chin?"

Gopal nodded, affirming the description of the sketch artist. Dubey had a concerned face as he glued his eyes on the blank white sheet standing just behind the sketch artist. The artist drew an outline of a square-shaped human face and glanced at Gopal for his opinion.

"A little lengthier," Gopal suggested.

"Then you should have said rectangular," the artist argued in frustration.

Every scratch of the pencil on that sheet increased Dubey's heartbeat. He had been praying that should turn out to be anyone's face, but not Abhimanyu's. A shrill, loud and weird ringtone broke the concentration of the sketch artist and startled Dubey. Gopal grinned, followed by an apologetic expression, and fetched his mobile out from his chest pocket.

"*Han bolo*," Gopal shouted, receiving the call. Dubey gestured him to lower his voice.

"Baba, your friends is here. When you are coming home?"

A pleasant smile lit Gopal's face hearing his daughter's faulty dialect. "You tell him to come back in the evening. Baba is busy now," he replied with a grin.

"Hello Gopal! I am the guy you are trying to describe to that sketch artist."

The grin lingered, leaving several wrinkles on Gopal's face as he heard Abhimanyu. Before he could respond, Abhimanyu added, "Don't say a word and listen to me very carefully. Your wife and daughter are absolutely safe and sound, till you identify me."

"What should I..."

"Shhhh... not a single word, just listen," Abhimanyu cut him off and continued, "Don't show any reluctance, help them with the same enthusiasm, but give them a different face."

"Can I talk to…" the call suddenly disconnected before Gopal could finish his words.

The sketch artist gazed at Dubey. It wasn't difficult for Dubey to comprehend his frustration. Dubey patted on his shoulder to calm him down and ordered one of the policemen to arrange for tea and samosa.

"Can we start?" Dubey asked while Gopal kept his mobile back in his chest pocket.

Gopal nodded reluctantly.

After an hour of Gopal's misleading description and honest effort of that sketch artist, a face appeared on that white paper, a bald and pulpy face with a bandage on his head. In the meanwhile, Vayu and Chaddha had reached there.

"But I remember you telling me that he looks like a hero," Vayu asked, staring at the sketch.

"Anupam Kher *bhi toh hero ka role kiya hai*," Gopal replied nervously.

Vayu glanced at Dubey, Chaddha and the sketch artist seeking some reference as he had heard that name for the first time in his life.

"He is a Bollywood actor," Dubey answered.

"Is there any kind of pressure on you, Mr Gopal?" Vayu enquired as he could clearly read his unusually stiff body language.

Gopal shook his head and requested, "Let me go, sir. I haven't opened my shop since morning."

They had to let him go.

However, Vayu wasn't convinced with that sketch and advised Dubey, "Don't waste your time searching for this man in the sketch; it's fictional. Keep digging further."

He murmured thoughtfully after some moments of silence, "This is something bigger than our imagination. Something is terribly wrong. I can smell it, but can't see."

"Yes, do we have any pattern?" Abhimanyu asked his subordinate in the cyber department without any greeting. His voice shook in impatience and curiosity.

"Yes sir. The locations are pretty much repetitive in the last few days; even the timings are the same. Other than a few random short-spanning locations, there are three major locations where the subject has spent most of the time. The first one is a lodge named Drive Inn as per Google maps, where the subject spends most the time in the day. It must be the workplace of the subject. Otherwise, who will spend only daytime in…"

"Leave the analysis to me. What are the other two locations?" Abhimanyu cut him off and asked edgily.

"Second one is a residential area in sector 15, and the third one is the most interesting, near an abandoned under-construction building in Greater Noida, sector MU–I. Subject spends almost the entire night in that debris of concrete."

"Thanks! I owe you big time. Just ask as per your convenience."

Abhimanyu had a hint of relief on his face as he lit the cigarette and inhaled a lengthy puff. It was only six in the evening when he left the police station to prepare for the hunt that night.

Vayu's next attempt to reach Shanaya's lawyer went in vain as the call got disconnected after a full ring; that was his sixth attempt since afternoon. He reached home, freshened up, and started watching Shanaya's next session with Dr Rahul.

"I didn't miss any opportunity of being alone at home with him. Eventually, I started hanging around with Alex outdoor as well. That relation of the real world stripped my addiction to virtual people and self-gratification. I didn't need to describe someone else's body as mine any longer, hiding behind my keyboard. Alex could see and touch the real me in flesh and blood.

"However, our relation couldn't survive for more than a month. One day, Papa returned home quite early while Ba had gone out shopping. He always had a spare key with him. Papa opened the main door with that key without ringing the doorbell, entered home, and finally reached my room after searching the entire house for any of us. He stood there like a statue for a few seconds while he found us naked on the bed. He silently left the room and when Alex went out of the room after wearing his clothes, he ordered, 'Go home and bring your father right now!'

"Papa was a progressive man. But I know that it was quite too much for a father to digest right away. He didn't get into an argument with Alex's father, just informed him about the situation, paid him for whatever the work had been done then, and asked them to leave forever."

"Did he punish you?" Dr Khanna asked.

"No, he never punished me by any means in his entire life. He just gave lengthy advice and the bottom-line was that I should wisely choose people in my life. I should use my brain instead of heart to guide me in that. Until today, I don't know what was wrong in choosing Alex as my life partner."

"I think it's his financial and social status."

"But why was Alex's financial and social status so important to my father? Wasn't that my responsibility as well? I could have given Alex a better life after marriage. Didn't Papa have confidence in me that I could earn in the future? Why is it necessary for a woman to be dependent on a stable man? What if I would have been a male and Alex a female? Still, do you think Papa would have been worried about my girlfriend's financial and social status?" Shanaya asked, frowning.

"It's our social conviction to judge everyone on the same scale. But that scale differs with gender. Earning is the scale to judge a male, whereas tolerance and obedience of social norms is the scale for a female. I am not supporting this mechanism, just stating a fact," Dr Khanna replied.

He paused the video as his mobile started buzzing on the centre table in front of him. He breathed a sigh of relief with a pleasant smile on his face when he saw the name Sunil Jha on the screen.

"May I know who this is? There are so many missed calls in my call history from this number," Sunil asked as Vayu accepted the call.

"This is Vayu Iyer from Noida police station."

"Oh, yes! Someone from your department had already reached out to me for Shanaya's murder case."

"Yes, sir. I was trying to reach you for the same. I just want to know the names of people who would financially benefit after Shanaya's death," Vayu asked, strolling around his drawing-room restlessly.

"Your department will get an elaborate mail from my office with all the details about Shanaya's will by tomorrow morning before ten o'clock."

"That'll be great, sir. But it would be of immense help if you could tell me just the names over the phone. I am the investigating officer for that homicide. We are under pressure to conclude this investigation well before the election, and we are literally running out of time." Vayu requested.

"I am sorry; that's not how it works," Sunil replied and disconnected the call.

Vayu thrashed the phone on the couch in frustration for a moment and resumed his video.

"How did you deal with that break-up? I believe you must have invested a lot of emotions and true feelings on the first man in your life; that's quite certain for any human," Dr Khanna asked.

"Yes, I did, and that incident pushed me to a prolonged depression…"

Shanaya continued talking about her journey through that rough phase of her life and how time had healed her eventually. Vayu kept watching, regulating the tempo of the video as per his judgement of importance.

Abhimanyu lit his tenth cigarette while waiting for his prey at the exact location in greater Noida, sector MU–I. The name, Ghost City, perfectly suited that area. Hundreds of abandoned unfinished buildings spread across miles. It looked like an apocalyptic wasteland or a movie set of sorts for a post-disaster scene. In those streets between those tall buildings, he was the only beating heart. Due to legal complications, builders had stopped working on those skyscrapers, and since then, time had stopped there. A gust of dry wind blew through the maze of those buildings where windows had long shattered in the weakness of their structures. Doors hung on hinges and groaned with pain at every sway. Abhimanyu heard a pale sound of a bike. He threw the cigarette butt in a hurry, wore his pair of gloves, groped on his tool pouch apron around his waist confirming that all the weapons were perfectly placed according to his convenience and hid behind a collapsed wall. He wore a lengthy, black raincoat to get rid of any bloodstain on his clothes and that tool pouch apron was wrapped around his waist on top of that raincoat. However, he wasn't wearing any mask because except him, there was only one species with warm blood, flesh and a beating heart in that dark jungle of concrete, iron and wood. And that was his prey.

Eventually, the faint sound of that bike-engine turned into a sharp thumping and muted after rattling noise. The clang of the bike's stand followed by the sound of footsteps offered Abhimanyu a vivid gumption of the situation at the other side of that collapsed wall. Gradually, the sound of that footsteps started fading away. He took his boots off, came out from behind the wall, and started following the sound of footsteps. He couldn't hear those footsteps anymore after reaching the fourth floor. He hopped on the floor to reach the nearest pillar from the staircase landing and stepped on a nail. He screamed in pain for a split second before grabbing his mouth to hush himself up. However, the damage had been done. His scream had alerted the quarry by then, and his quarry set out for hunting the hunter.

Abhimanyu sat on the floor behind that pillar and unbuttoned the raincoat till his waist from the bottom. He started hearing those footsteps again all around that floor. He held his wounded right leg, folded it in a hurry, and placed it on his left thigh. That nail wasn't visible in the darkness. He lightly rubbed his finger around that portion where he had been feeling an intolerable pain. He held the nail's head in a pinch and tugged it with a jerk. Blood gushed forth from his feet. Absence of walls made the sky visible from the floor where Abhimanyu was sitting and the sudden arrival of a human silhouette, keeping the glowing sky at its back, startled him. Before he could comprehend anything, the silhouette swung a metal rod aiming at his face. He stooped in time, and that rod hit the pillar. Small chunks of cement came off the pillar along with dust. Abhimanyu straightened his wounded right leg and kicked that man with his left leg while lying on the ground, before he could strike for the second time with his rod. That silhouette lost his balance and fell on the ground. Abhimanyu jumped on him like a cheetah and grabbed his neck. That man put up a fight to get his control back, but he couldn't move anymore. Abhimanyu fetched out a piece of cloth from his tool pouch apron with his unengaged hand and pressed it on that man's face. It took almost five minutes for that chloroform-soaked cloth to turn that man into a breathing dead.

"Sometimes, a single incident in our life changes everything in a blink before we comprehend the conspiracy behind it. Apparently, that single incident doesn't influence every aspect of our life, but the rippling effect of that incident keeps triggering other similar incidents. Like someone throws a pebble in a tranquil puddle. I am not saying these propagative events always bring negativity in our lives. But in my case, that single incident had invited a prolonged nightmare for me. Everything changed that night. It smashed the shield of numbness I had made around me to keep myself away from emotions, relationships, expectations and agonies. And that was just the beginning of it," Shanaya murmured.

She spoke so softly that Vayu had to concentrate hard to hear her clearly.

Shanaya continued after clearing her throat, "A few months after Alex's departure, Papa also left us. He suffered a heart stroke. After his demise, we went through a horrible financial crunch. His scrawny pension wasn't enough to sustain the lifestyle we were so used to. Unexpectedly bitten by poverty, we were compelled to cut off our expenses which we could survive without. Not only that, we also fooled ourselves by labelling a few of our essentials as luxuries and chopped them off. I started giving tuitions to some kids in our neighbourhood. But that crisis was much darker and deeper than our efforts. Compelled by circumstances, Ba started working in a garment factory. Her job helped us to absorb that storm a bit and gather the scattered pieces of our lives.

"It doesn't matter how brutal and adverse the circumstances are. Like it usually happens, time and the struggle for survival showed us how to beat all odds. Gradually, time healed us too.

"Yes, I regressed to the cyber world and self-gratification. It seemed much more consolatory as compared to the real world; no expectations, no pain in return. My happiness and pleasure were in my control, and my emotions were just a matter of a few buttons on the keyboard; no one could hurt me anymore.

"Almost one year passed like that. One day, Ba introduced me to a man in his late forties, Pranav Nischol, as her boss and friend. He was the owner of that garment factory, Nischol textile, where Ba had been working. With each passing day, his visits to our home became more frequent. I noticed Ba's joviality in his presence. She changed into a much younger woman when he was around. And after a few months, she asked my permission to marry Pranav Nischol. What could be my reason for opposing their relationship? After all, she seemed happy, and taking good care of herself. It seemed she had found a new meaning for her life... something like a fresh start. She was just thirty-seven then; too young to spend the rest of her life as a widow. I agreed. They got married, and Pranav Nischol's bungalow became our new home.

"Mr Nischol seemed like a good man; he used to take good care of my mother. And that was all I could expect from him. However, I never could call him Papa because that word 'Papa' has only one irreplaceable face for me. My conversation with him always remained formal, repetitive and limited to a few words.

"But, I just didn't like how his eyes lingered on my accidentally exposed cleavage, my bare legs whenever I wore shorts or any other unclothed part of my body. I ignored all that initially, for the sake of Ba's happiness.

"Everything had been falling into place perfectly, and that scared me. I was not pessimistic by birth. but life had taught me that when everything seems like cakewalk, it's just an advent song of a brutal and gloomy devil; in the form of a human or an incident.

"I was busy preparing for my higher secondary board examinations. One day while I was changing clothes in my room, my eyes met another pair of eyes. The door was ajar, and they were peeping through it. I felt a chill through my spine as I moved aside to the corner of the room. I could feel my raging heart and adrenaline rush in my body. It wasn't difficult for me to recognize that familiar disgusting gaze of Mr Nischol.

"I thought of speaking with Ba about that incident several times, but eventually changed my mind. The thorns of dilemma had been tearing away at my core. Anyway, I finally thought a lot and made up my mind to keep my mouth shut. Unfortunately, my silence encouraged him, and he started finding lame excuses to touch me indecently.

"Eventually, I started spending most of my time outside the house and made sure Ba was around whenever I had to stay home."

Shanaya smirked and said, "It was like a never-ending game of hide and seek. However, my strategies had been working perfectly."

She continued, "Another year passed. My heart had been a mess until I met Rizwan Ahmed in college. I had gone into a mode of denial and refusal. I had shut my mind and soul for any new relationship. So, I had turned down his proposal initially, but he never gave up on me. He was happy to be around me selflessly, like a shadow, without any kind of demand. I didn't find any reason to oppose him. He already had two of his school friends in the same class, Supriya and Sandy. Eventually, I became a part of that pack of friends. We started hanging around the city almost every day, bunking classes, watching movies and going to restaurants, pubs, discos and where not. Sometimes, we used to footle the whole day by some railway tracks or by a silent lake. I felt like my wounds had been healing in their companionship, and I started enjoying my life once again," Shanaya spoke in her usual lazy style of talking and mused in a nostalgic trip to her college days.

Vayu increased the television volume as he couldn't afford to miss any word from that portion onwards.

"Rizwan was quite attractive, the centre of attention for all the girls in our batch, and he had been waiting for me." Shanaya paused momentarily and said, smiling, "So pleasing to know, isn't it? However, more than his striking physique and charming face, the tranquillity of his mind even in strained circumstances, strong personality and dependability got the best of me. He was the kind of guy you would want on your side, you know. It looked like he had some mystic powers, some blessing that safeguarded him in any adverse scenario. His dreamy, deep eyes were my cocoon of comfort.

"One day, when we all came out of the college campus, the sky was a monochromatic image of its daytime beauty, painted in black and white, with clouds swirling like spilled black ink in water. That was unusual weather in winter. The winter breeze was piercing, thanks to the temperature dropping by a few degrees."

"Rizwan said, looking at the sky, 'It will rain heavily'. Though it seemed like a general statement for all of us, I could sense his intention was to draw my attention.

"Sandy had been staying in the college hostel just to get rid of his nagging parents. He high-fived with us left quickly, breaking our usual habit of hanging out for a couple of more hours on campus after the classes. He wanted to reach his room before it started raining. Rizwan had a bike, and usually, he used to drop off Supriya at her home on their way back, as they lived close by. And my home was in a completely different direction. However, that day, Rizwan made an excuse for some personal work and convinced Supriya to hire an auto.

"Rizwan offered after Supriya left, 'It won't be wise to board public transport now. I can drop you if you want.' I looked into his eyes for a few seconds and nodded my affirmation on an impulse.

"It started pouring on the way and drenched us completely. My wet and heavy warm clothing, the chilled weather and the wind splashing raindrops on my face made me shiver on the back seat of Rizwan's bike. Obviously, Rizwan had been tolerating more.

"Hide yourself behind me and sit closer, holding me tightly. It will give you a bit of comfort," Rizwan shouted, turning his head back and accelerating his bike's speed. I obeyed him as if I was under his spell. I loved the fragrance of his perfume locked inside the twill of his wet sweater and the warmth of his body. I could feel his racing heartbeats on my palms as I wrapped my arms around his chest. I rested my head on his back and closed my eyes. I had really felt safe and secured, as if I was at home. I wished I could pause time forever, hoping this journey never ended.

"When we reached closer to my home, I noticed a small crowd near the gate from a distance. I couldn't see anything but their umbrellas; most of them were black, except a few in different colours. I couldn't think of any delightful reason for that crowd. I felt a deep hollowness in my chest. I got off the bike in a hurry after Rizwan stopped the bike at the opposite side of the road, and rushed towards that crowd. I heard Rizwan's voice behind me, but his words couldn't grab my attention. All my senses were rushing towards that unknown misfortunate inside my home. I felt my legs becoming heavier with each step. I made my way towards the entrance, pushing the crowd aside.

A few words from their discussion pierced my ears and made my eyes blur in tears.

"I stared straight at our domestic help's eyes, reaching the dining hall. My arrival made her weaker, and she burst into tears. She was sitting on the floor. I knew that the woman lying on the floor, resting her head on her lap was Ba. But I had no courage to look at her. I spent close to a minute gazing at the house help with a lot of hope in my eyes. I so badly expected her to say that everything was alright, and there was nothing serious. I couldn't make sense of anything. Moreover, Mr Nischol was on a business trip to Mumbai."

Shanaya's voice became heavy. The words choked in her throat, and she failed to continue talking any further. Tears rolled down on her cheeks. She mopped her face with a handkerchief.

"Take your time," Dr Khanna advised.

After drinking a few sips of water, she continued, "Ba had slipped on the wet floor of the bathroom. She severely injured her neck and the back of the head. The pain had almost pushed her to the point of blacking out; maybe it would have been easier for her to lose consciousness. One of our neighbours in that gathering informed me that they had already called an ambulance. However, it was stuck in a huge traffic jam due to the heavy rain.

"I could think of only one person whom I believed to be my saviour – Rizwan. I hadn't seen him helping anyone in such a critical scenario. I didn't know anything about him or his connects, that could pull me out of that jeopardy. But a blind conviction got the best of me, and I rushed back to the street. Somewhere in my heart, I believed that he would be waiting for me. And when I came out of the house, I could see my guardian angel waiting for me at the same spot where I had left him.

"I updated him on what had happened and he called one of his friends who lived nearby to seek his help. His friend arrived in front of my home in the next three minutes with an eight-seater Innova. With the help of our neighbours, Rizwan, his friend and I laid Ba on the car's back seat and rushed towards the nearest hospital. I sat on the vehicle's floor, holding Ba's head on the seat with Rizwan.

"Rizwan stayed with me that whole night in the hospital. Our wet clothes had dried by then, but my heart was drenched in love and admirations for him."

The clock showed two in the morning. Vayu switched off the television and walked towards the bedroom.

Mukund woke up, tired and groggy. He tried to open his eyelids, but failed. He flickered them for a few seconds before shutting them again completely. He felt the fluid that was rolling down behind his left ear. It smelt like blood. He couldn't feel anything other than the pain at the back of his head. He was a man of average build with curly hair, a beard, a ring in one of his ears and tattoos on his throat, forearms and neck.

"Wake up, your highness!" He heard a faint voice.

"Whe...where am I?" Mukund murmured. He couldn't hear any voice in return but heard the clang of a metal bucket. And to his surprise, he felt a hefty splash of water on his face. He opened his mouth wide to gasp some air for breathing, but gulped some water instead.

"Sir, wake up! Your breakfast is getting cold."

It wasn't difficult for him to recognise Abhimanyu's voice. He heard each of his words clearly. As the water washed out the numbness of his body, he could sense his hands were tied together at his back, and his legs were helplessly fastened with the front two legs of that chair he had been sitting on. He opened eyes to a blurry vision, but he could identify that place easily. He looked around and fixed his eyes on Abhimanyu.

"So, this is the place? Your den, huh?" Abhimanyu said, sitting on his haunches in front of Mukund with a moan. The wound on his foot was becoming intolerable with time.

It was kind of a tent, erected at the corner of the fourth floor, made of a huge polythene sheet, a few jute sacs and bedsheets held up by two ropes, wrapped around two of the nearest pillars. Abhimanyu limped around the tent.

"Wow! A well-equipped playground, I must say," Abhimanyu said confidently, having a thorough look all over that tent. "So, these are the devices which have stolen the peace of my mind." He mused as he examined the gadgets, plied at the corner of that tent – one laptop, two camcorders, one external DVD writer, several CDs, and many more tiny gismos.

His attention returned to Mukund, who was staring at him through his partly opened pair of eyes and asked, "Do you have a team, or do you handle this extortion business alone?"

"Alone."

Abhimanyu nodded with an appreciative expression, picked up those CDs, and asked, "You record the intimate moments of those couples who come to your lodge, make these CDs, and then... do you sell them in the market or blackmail them?"

"It depends on the people who are there on the video," Mukund murmured, his head hanging from his shoulder.

"Huh! I got it...I got it, business prospect. So, you blackmail the rich couples and sell the others. But how do you classify them? After all, all humans fuck in the same way; rich or poor," Abhimanyu enquired, throwing that CD back to its pile. He picked up the laptop and staggered close to him.

"I do a background check on them after they leave the motel," Mukund answered.

"Wow! That's impressive," Abhimanyu appreciated, slapping him on the back of his head where he had the wound. Mukund screamed.

"Okay, enough of the chitchat. Now, tell me all the passwords to get into your inbox and delete the mail that you have scheduled."

Abhimanyu switched on the laptop to its login screen and held that in front of Mukund.

Mukund started laughing, pushing Abhimanyu to the edge of his tolerance. Abhimanyu waited till the end of his laughter, smiling.

"Do you think I will ruin all my hard work so easily?" Mukund taunted, continuing his laugh. A few seconds later, getting control over his laugh, he said, "I know you can't kill me until you stop that e-mail. Don't make it tough for both of us. Just get me the money and close the deal; it's easy."

"If I wanted to kill you, I would have done that within one hour of your first call," Abhimanyu said, keeping the laptop aside and adding, "I know I can't do that. But death is much easier than staying alive, particularly when you are sitting in front of Abhimanyu Rathore, tied to a chair."

Abhimanyu fetched out an extraction forceps from his tool pouch apron, held that firmly in his right hand, and said softly, "Normally, people beg for death in that situation."

"Wha...What is that?" Mukund fumbled after a certain comprehension of Abhimanyu's intentions.

Abhimanyu smiled and said, "It's a small tool; it always comes handy for breaking arrogant people."

He sat on the floor close to Mukund's feet who was groaning with a contorted face, grabbed Mukund's right foot, and said calmly, "I will pluck out your nails one by one; all twenty of them, if needed. Just tell me the password whenever you want me to stop."

Mukund started pushing the backrest of the chair violently to free himself from the bondage and cried loudly, "No! No!"

That quadruped wooden chair couldn't bear that jerk and toppled over. Mukund continued his fight to freedom lying on the floor. Abhimanyu tightened his grasp over his right leg, held the thumbnail in the pinch of that forceps, and tugged it aggressively. Mukund screamed, followed by a loud cry. Tears streamed out along with some saliva. Though that nail wasn't detached completely from his thumb, he was bleeding heavily.

Abhimanyu reached the corner of the tent, dragging himself on the floor, rested his back on the wall, and lit a cigarette. He took a lengthy puff gazing at Mukund, who had been fidgeting in intolerable pain like a beheaded sacrificial beast. Mukund strained against his body to break the wooden chair, testing his endurance.

Abhimanyu wondered whether something was wrong with his eyes, savouring Mukund as if he was an entertainment. He liked to see Mukund, watching his own blood flow, and his screams seemed like music, the finest and the most raw instrument he'd ever heard. The remorse that he felt after killing Oorja was not there anymore. He mused, 'Who am I, a monster? Where is that primitive drive with which I had started off, to bring justice for Ahi? Why am I enjoying my victims' suffering, savouring their pain and helplessness? Somewhere in my mind, I have disrupted the threshold of humanity, guilt and emotions. Now, I am addicted to hunting.'

He raised himself on his feet with the support of the wall, limped down to Mukund, and whispered, "Password or another nail?"

Mukund kept slurring the passwords one by one, moaning, and led Abhimanyu to his inbox. Abhimanyu deleted that scheduled mail.

"Any other scheduling?" Abhimanyu enquired.

Mukund shook his head and pleaded, "Now, please let me go! You will never see me again, I promise."

Abhimanyu straightened the chair on the floor along with Mukund and said, "Sure." He pulled out a knife from his tool pouch apron, cut the rope around Mukund's legs, and went behind Mukund to free his hands. But instead of the rope, he slit his throat in a blink.

Abhimanyu wrapped all those gadgets and CDs in a jute sack and stared for home. It was 4 a.m. The sun had just started rising in the sky, along with the darkness of a monster in Abhimanyu's heart and soul.

"Do we have any e-mail or fax or any kind of communication from Shanaya's lawyer?" Vayu enquired Chaddha immediately after reaching the police station.

Chaddha shook his head in the negative.

Vayu glanced at his wristwatch and murmured, "It's 9.45; still fifteen minutes to go."

"*Chalo, chai peeke aate hain, samose ke sath,*" Chaddha proposed as he stood up from the chair and pulled the waist of his trousers over his bulged-out stomach, stopping it from sliding down.

Vayu shook his head, chuckling and said, "Chaddha *ji*, take care of your fitness a bit. Who eats samosas in the morning?"

Chaddha sat back on the chair with a sullen expression. In the meanwhile, an e-mail arrived followed by ding of notification. Chaddha opened it in no time. Vayu leaned over the monitor, and both started reading.

"I don't understand. So much of beating around the bush. What is the bottom line?" Chaddha asked, sighing after gluing his eyes to the monitor for a few minutes.

"It says that Shanaya has donated almost forty percent of her property to different charitable trusts, and the rest of the property has been divided equally between her husband Manoj, and her sister Poonam," Vayu said, sticking his eyes on the monitor.

"So, Dr Khanna is not our guy?" Chaddha sounded worried and disheartened.

Vayu nodded in affirmation, took his eyes off from the monitor, and stood there like a statue. After a few minutes, he muttered, "We are going nowhere!" Spending a few more minutes in that state of mind, he said, "It's strange that there is no mention of Nischol Textile in her will."

"Shanaya is not the owner of Nischol Textile. She just had a power of attorney to take any business decisions on behalf of Poonam. Poonam is the sole inheritor of Nischol Textiles," Chaddha informed with a lot of pride as he knew something that Vayu didn't.

"Hmm! A stepfather with no exception," Vayu remarked sighing and asked, "Don't we have briefing with Abhimanyu today?"

Chaddha nodded.

"Abhimanyu will eat me up; he won't leave this opportunity. Have you seen him in the office, by the way?" Vayu enquired.

"Not yet," Chaddha said, getting up from the chair and suggested, "Let's make a plan over a cup of tea."

Vayu smiled, shaking his head.

"You had been asking for that Awasthi's script, right?" Chaddha asked on the way to the tea stall. He fetched out his mobile from his pocket, showed a number to Vayu, and said, "There is no sign of that script anywhere any longer. No clue whatsoever, except for this mobile number."

"Whose is this?" Vayu asked after saving the number in his mobile.

"Mohammad Samim Chaudhary, Ahi's close friend and partner in her publication. Have you heard of the news channel, Prime Time?"

Vayu nodded.

"He is the face of that channel, a celebrity newsreader. Though the chances are very thin that he will have a copy of it and will be ready to give it to you, but you can try."

"*Chaar garam samosa de aur do cup chai, jaldi se!*" Chaddha shouted instantly after reaching the teashop.

It was impossible for Abhimanyu to ride his bike with his wounded foot. So he hired a cab to reach the police station. Even the extra layering of cotton inside the bandage and tough sole of his service boots couldn't defeat the pain, especially when he had to bear his body weight on that wounded foot. Though his doctor had advised him to use a crutch until it healed completely, his devil-may-care attitude got the best of him.

Chaddha came down to him as he entered the police station hobbling and asked, "What happened, sir?"

Abhimanyu chuckled and said, "Nothing, just a small wound."

Chaddha helped him to walk up to his cabin and settle on his chair.

"Do you need anything?" Chaddha asked.

"No, I am fine. Call Vayu, and let's have a discussion on our investigation. That's why I am here. Otherwise, I would have taken a leave today," Abhimanyu said taking a sip of water from the glass which was kept on the table and sighed.

Chaddha left and returned along with Vayu after a couple of minutes. They occupied two of the chairs as Abhimanyu gestured them to have a seat.

"So, where are we?" Abhimanyu asked, leaning back on his chair.

"We have found some bottles of blended essential oils in Shanaya's bedroom. Our lab is yet to send the formal reports, but they verbally confirmed the existence of ricin in each of them. Those bottles seemed homemade to me with handwritten labels on them. The names of the primary oils were used to create that mixture written in those tags. I was quite sure that…."

"Can we just cut the craps and talk only about what we have found? I am not interested in the how part," Abhimanyu interrupted Vayu.

Vayu became silent and gulped down the rest of his thoughts about what he had decided to speak about. Chaddha lowered his head to evade any eye contact with either of them.

Vayu took a few more moments of silence to gather his thoughts and said, "Okay," sighing and continued, "So, it was Dr Khanna who gave Shanaya those bottles for better sleep and reduced anxiety. And the statement of Shanaya's domestic help Manju confirms that fact."

"Then what are we waiting for?" Abhimanyu asked, shrugging. He abandoned his laid-back disposition on the chair, leaned over the table, and ordered softly, "Prepare all the documents, arrest him and update me immediately after the arrest. Do it today; the entire nation has been waiting for an answer."

"But Abhi... I am sorry, I mean, sir, I am not sure about his motive to murder Shanaya. We have checked Shanaya's will and found only Shanaya's husband and sister. Dr Khanna is not a beneficiary. Moreover, Dr Khanna has many such rich and influential clients. She was no special," Vayu argued.

"That's not our job, Mr FBI. Let the court decide all that. We are here to collect evidence and make an arrest as suggested by those evidences," Abhimanyu mocked and leaned back, pushing the backrest of his chair to the semi-sleeper position.

After a few moments of silence, Abhimanyu said, "I don't understand your logic, Vayu. There might be a hell lot of other motives to kill a person. Why are we looking for only the beneficiaries of her wealth? Even if I consider that's the only motive, isn't it possible that Shanaya's husband appointed or teamed up with Dr Khanna to kill her in exchange for some shares of her wealth?"

"In that case, Shanaya's husband wouldn't have left those bottles in her bedroom till today," Vayu replied.

"Maybe that's his plan of betraying Dr Khanna and taking away all the money. And what about her sister? It could be her plan as well," Abhimanyu snapped back.

"Poonam is the sole owner of her father's property. So a monetary angle doesn't suit her. Moreover, she used to admire, respect and love Shanaya. After the death of Poonam's parents in her childhood, Shanaya became her parent, teacher, guide and support system. I don't see any motive there as well," Vayu argued softly but steadily.

"Okay! But I don't think you have enough logical argument for her husband and Dr Khanna's teaming up theory. Do you?" Abhimanyu enquired.

"Her husband gave us Dr Khanna's address in the first place. Otherwise, we never could have found those shades of Shanaya's life." Vayu wasn't ready to give up.

"As I said before, that might be his plan to get rid of Dr Khanna," Abhimanyu snapped back and waited for Vayu's response.

Vayu had no answer for that. Silence conquered the room until Abhimanyu repeated his order, "Then arrest him today and update me immediately."

Dr Rahul Khanna had been arrested. Police sealed his office and seized all his communication devices. The cybercrime department had started digging into his virtual world to find his connection with Shanaya's husband.

DGP Omprakash Bakshi held a press conference the same evening. He briefed the case in detail, appreciating the investigating officers Abhimanyu and Vayu, along with constables Chaddha, Dubey and other policemen. Moreover, that conference was the answer to all the criticisms and humiliation against the Noida police department. There had been a wind of pride and glory that brushed each employee's heart and soul. They gathered in front of the television in the cafeteria and applauded in unison after every word of appreciation from Omprakash Bakshi in the press conference. Chaddha couldn't hide his pride and pleasure when he saw the expressions of his colleagues as Omprakash Bakshi mentioned his name on TV. Dubey joined him in celebration.

However, Abhimanyu returned home from the police station like a regular day, refusing Omprakash's invitation to attend the press conference. He was completely apathetic to those celebrations as he switched off his mobile and started snorting the lines of white powder.

There was only one man who wasn't happy about the conclusion of that investigation – Vayu Iyer. His rational thought had bothered him as he had been watching the press conference from a distant corner of the cafeteria.

"He has no motive!" Vayu mused, taking a sip of his coffee.

Shanaya had been talking about her college days when her world used to revolve around Rizwan. And Vayu glued his eyes on the television screen, completely zoned out. His mind rushed through his memory lanes, revisiting all those moments of interrogating Rizwan, Jignesh, Manoj and Dr Khanna. He wondered whether he had missed anything to observe in their expressions, body language, gestures and choice of words. "It would have been suicide for both of us" – those words of Rizwan, "These motherfuckers have never been my friends" –Jignesh's comment, Supriya's testimony – "Shanaya slapped Jignesh after reading it, crumpled the paper, threw it on his face in front our whole class" and that compulsion of Manoj – "She did help me several times, but not this time" were popping up in his mind.

All of them had a strong motive to kill Shanaya, the failed attempt of recuperating the lost love, revenge, self-preservation and greed. Vayu wondered what Dr Khanna's motive might be. Or Abhimanyu was right, and he had been living in denial.

"I broke up with Rizwan during the final year of my college." Vayu heard Shanaya's voice, and those words brought his attention back to the television screen.

"Why?" Dr Khanna asked. Vayu picked the remote and increased the volume.

"Rizwan was always by my side during those days. It had happened several times that I gave vent to all my unreasonable frustration and anger by yelling at Rizwan. But I always returned home with a smile on my face. He was such a charmer who could soak all my negative energies. I had never seen his anger, except on two occasions. Once when one of our college mates, Jignesh, gave me an indecent letter, and the second when he found a hidden camera in Sandy's room."

Shanaya said in embarrassment, "Yes, we used to make out in Sandy's hostel room quite often. Sandy deleted all the recordings in front of Rizwan and promised him that it won't be repeated." After a few seconds of silence, she muttered, smiling, "He was my guardian angel."

"Then, why did you break up?" Dr Khanna repeated his question.

"Yeah! Why?" Vayu shouted impatiently.

Shanaya continued, "After one day of Ba's hospitalization, she slipped into a coma. She was completely unconscious. In the couple of weeks that followed, she had recovered to a vegetative state from unconsciousness. She appeared to be responding better to family members than to strangers. I started spending most of my time with her in the hospital. The doctor advised me to show her our family photo album and identify the people incorrectly in those pictures, so that she would try to correct me. I was advised to piece together at least eight important stories or concerning events that we took part in together as a family. I needed to bring the stories to life with sensations, hand gestures, expressions and movement. And during all those days of struggle, Rizwan was there like my backbone. He had been helping me rehearse those stories so that I could present them in a livelier way in front of Ba.

"It took almost four months but she started responding to our voices. Though just by the movement of her eyeballs. She could just hear and see us.

"Since the day of Ba's hospitalization, I had been noticing a drastic change in her husband's behaviour. He seemed more concerned about his expenses for the treatment rather than Ba's health, and after a few more weeks, he announced his decision to stop the treatment. That day is still vivid in my mind when I went into his room and literally begged him for continuing Ba's treatment.

"He had been relishing a ghazal on his stereo with delayed and lazy sips of whiskey. That was his leisure time pass after returning home from the factory. He reduced the volume with the remote after listening to my pitiful longing and asked me to sit on the couch in front of him. 'Listen, I spent my childhood in extreme poverty as my parents were just daily wagers. Hunger was my toy to play with all the time. We never had a permanent roof over our heads; spent most of my life in temporary shelters by the construction sites, spent innumerable sleepless nights in a wet bed due to the rain and spent many winters without any warm clothes,' he said, playing with the floating ice cubes in his whisky. 'So, that should make you kinder to the people in need. And moreover, she is your wife. It's your responsibility, not any charity.' I made my statement.

"He said, 'That rough phase taught me one lesson – that nothing is free in this world. Either you should have the ability to buy, or the power to snatch. Everything in my life is a business deal, including relationships. It might not always be in exchange for money, but I exchange something like security, status, shelter, respect, happiness and few selective emotions.' He rose from the chair, walked up to the open window, took a sip of his whisky and continued, "I gave fifty years of my life to build this empire brick by brick. But lately, I have realised that I should savour my hard work, money and power. Your mother was in my mind ever since I saw her for the first time in my office. A beautiful and attractive young widow from a decent background. I could have bought some younger whores as well. But sex in exchange of money is not my cup of tea. Moreover, they might carry some diseases, who knows!"

"I couldn't believe my ears. 'So, my mother is just a sex toy for you, a machine to get you an heir?' I snapped back in disgust. He looked at me and said softly, "Come on! It wasn't a bad deal at all. A poor widow got a shelter for herself and her daughter along with the expense of education, medical treatment, clothing, food, entertainment and social status in exchange for giving birth to my child.'

"All my predetermined arguments and reasoning clogged inside my brain and I ran out of words. I was just a college student whose mother had been in a coma for the last six months. I was literally left with no option other than convincing that selfish man for Ba's treatment. I felt like someone had pushed me into deep water, and I was frail enough to swim. My head was pounding, every cell in my body was screaming for oxygen. 'Is there any way other than seeing her die?' I asked as a spontaneous reaction to the fright that conglomerated in the core of my senses. 'Every problem has a solution. You can pursue the unfinished job of your mother and keep my deal alive,' he proposed calmly as he returned to his rocking chair and lounged on it.

"I just couldn't tolerate that man anymore. I felt the heat on the tip of my nose and earlobes as I stormed out of that room in silence."

There was a silence on the TV screen. As much as Shanaya tried to hold it in, the pain came out like an uproar from her throat in the form of a silent scream. The beads of water started dripping one after another, without a sign of stopping. The muscles of her chin trembled like a small child. However, she didn't weep, sob or wipe the tears.

She had no wobbliness in her voice as she continued, "I was acquainted with the fact that none of my relatives would agree to bear that expense. But still, I reached out to each of them, and the result met my expectation. All the doors of hope had been closing on my face one by one."

After a silent moment, she smirked and said, "I was so immature and stupid then. I had a strong belief that my guardian angel would definitely pull me out of that quicksand which is why I proposed him to marry me. Obviously, he refused. Rizwan was just like me, a college student. I didn't break up with him because he couldn't stand by me when I needed him the most. Undoubtedly, it was a big ask for him at that moment. I broke up because it was meaningless to continue that relationship. Plus, I had no other option but to surrender myself to that monster for Ba's treatment.

"In the meanwhile, Ba had been released from the hospital with a lot of medication and instructions. Mr Nischol furnished a room wholeheartedly with all imported medical equipment for Ba as he had learnt about my unanimity in his deal. There was a convertible electrical patient bed, an alarm system with a remote, a television fixed at a higher position on the wall, an air conditioner, an arrangement for handling her waste materials, a nurse and a bed for the nurse.

"Ba had pride and pleasure in her eyes for her new husband as she entered that room on a stretcher. That was worth ruining my life for."

Shanaya became mute for a few seconds and looked out of the window.

"It's okay, we can continue tomorrow."

"No, Rahul, I just gathered all my courage to pour it all today. Maybe tomorrow I can't do it again," Shanaya replied, wiping her tears, which left stains on her cheeks.

Vayu observed that Shanaya had addressed Dr Khanna by his name and murmured, "Interesting!"

She resumed, "I was sitting at the edge of my bed, staring at the dark sky. It had rained heavily in the last two days and it looked like it could start again any minute. The dark clouds rolled across the sky, but no rain fell. Off in the distance, I could see small stars, twinkling and shining. And as the clouds parted, the moon became visible. It was a full moon, large and beautiful. The moonbeams filled my bedroom and washed everything in their silvery glow.

"Two days had passed since Ba returned home. I had spent those nights sitting at that same spot of my bed, waiting for that monster's call. Somehow, I started connecting my fate with that murky and overcast sky. And when those gloomy clouds departed allowing the moon to shine like a beacon of hope, I thought he might have changed his mind and might not be thirsty for my flesh anymore.

"My mobile started vibrating just then, and it triggered a chilling wave through my spinal cord. It must be him, I thought. But it was a call from Rizwan. I stopped the vibration and tossed it back on the bed. Rizwan must have thought that I was a selfish woman who used him. He didn't know my side of the story. And I wanted him to think likewise; it would help him to forget me quickly.

"My mobile started vibrating again. I picked up the phone, predetermined to insult Rizwan. However, the screen showed 'Nischol uncle'. He called me in his room. That bright full moon night was about to turn into the darkest night of my life.

"As usual, he had been savouring a ghazal with a glass of whisky in his hand on his favourite recliner. 'Take off your clothes,' he ordered without even looking at me as I entered the room. Despite all my mental preparation for that expected incident, I found myself shell-shocked, standing like a statue in the middle of that large room. Moreover, that room was flooded with lights, and that made me awfully uncomfortable. I kept standing there like a statue. 'Have you change your mind?' he asked, staring at me.

"I shook my head and muttered, 'Switch off the lights.' He said, 'Without seeing you, how can I turn my mood on? I am an old man, after all.' He sipped the whisky.

"I took my clothes off one by one as my whole body trembled in disgust and abashment. He kept staring at me as if I was some delicious food and slipped his hand inside his pyjama. His gaze on me froze my bones, like being nude in the middle of a hailstorm, where every chilled drop of rain was a frosted dagger cutting into the skin. I took my eyes away from him and glued them on one of the bright lights on the wall. After a couple of creepy minutes, he ordered, 'Come and sit on my lap.'

"I was mortified, frozen to that same spot on that soft carpet. I felt traumatized. My head began to spin as I took my first step towards him. I felt like all the walls, furniture and every single object in that room grew a pair of eyes and glued them on my naked body accompanied by that one living pair of eyes. My legs refused to move any further, but I kept pushing myself. I turned red in embarrassment like someone had whipped me and started radiating heat. He grabbed my hand, tugged me down, grabbed me by my waist, and made me sit in his lap. I was about to scream on an impulse, but I refrained myself, grabbing my mouth. I closed my eyes and allowed him to touch me everywhere without any protest. He started rubbing his face and tongue all over me like a large snake got hold of delicious prey. 'Get up!' he ordered in frustration. Few wrinkles of disgust replaced the boisterousness on his face. 'What?' was the only word I managed to speak as I rose from his lap. 'I am not able to engage my mind. Let's go to your mother's room. I need her face to bring my soul and heart in the act,' he said getting up from the chair.

"I almost screamed, 'That was not a part of the deal. I can't do it.' I covered my body as much as possible with my arms. 'Okay! So, let your mother die!' he said with a smirk. I had no answer. I stood there helplessly, feeling so vulnerable. He waited for my decision and finally said, 'I am considering your silence as your consensus. Let me ask that nurse to wait somewhere outside till we are done.'

"He left the room hurriedly, returned after a few minutes, and said, 'Let's go!' I kept standing there like a statue as my vision was blurred with tears. He grabbed my hand and dragged me towards Ba's room. I yanked my hands free from his grasp and stumbled around him, wanting to flee. He grabbed and lifted me on his lap from the floor. That nurse watched me naked, trying hard to free myself from that monster's grab in the hallway. He pushed open the door of Ba's room, switched on the light and flung me on the nurse's bed. I looked at Ba's face, hoping she remains asleep. She looked like an innocent kid, soaked in her fairy dreams. He took off his pyjama and rode me. My muscles stiffened in disgust as I closed my eyes and kept lying beneath him like a breathing ragdoll. Few minutes had passed, tolerating that obnoxious smell of whisky, sweat and semen along with his heavy weight on me. And then, when I opened my eyes to take another look at Ba, I saw her wide-open eyes. She had been looking at me. Tears rolled down from her eyes. Everything was finished."

Shanaya muted for a minute and told, "Fear is a strange emotion, isn't it? Until that incident happens, fear suffocates you. But, once you go through that incident, it vanishes from your mind and you turn into a courageous version of yourself. I saw my reflection on the metallic circle at the centre of that static fan hanging from the ceiling. The convex shape of it stretched the head of my reflection like a crown. I held eye contact with myself while he fucked me, slipping into some sort of twisted meditation. I considered myself someone else, a queen or a goddess and he was just some lowly subject I used for fun. There were guards in armour waiting outside my door and maidens who would bathe me and rub me with sweet-smelling oils before putting me to bed. That imagination was my only escape to retain my sanity.

"That inhumanity continued until I became pregnant. Ba died after a few months. I think she didn't want to live anymore.

"That was the first business deal of my life. I sold my dignity in an exchange of Ba's life."

"And where..."

"Poonam is my daughter from my stepfather," Shanaya answered before Dr Khanna could finish his predictable question.

"Many times, I thought of aborting the child. But I couldn't gather that courage to kill."

"What happened to your relationship with Rizwan?" Dr Khanna asked.

"That's all. We have been an incomplete sentence, a rhythmless poem, a half-written story... finished, without an ending," Shanaya murmured.

"Do you treat those random sex partners of yours as your slaves?"

Shanaya nodded a yes and said, "Initially, but not now."

"I see. That mishap is the trigger point of your life. You might think you have moved on in your life and that dark past doesn't bother you anymore. However, that humiliation is still fresh in your mind. And as you have been harbouring it for several years, it has twisted your psychology permanently. You slip into your stepfather's shoes whenever you engage in any sexual act. In your subconscious mind, you create the same scenario repetitively and try to win it repeatedly. Unlike your husband, you don't respect or love those casual flings. Sex is not a pleasure or part of love for you. For you, it's just a fight of winning back your broken pride," Dr Khanna explained.

Vayu switched off the television as he got the answers he had been looking for. He hit the hay at the crack of dawn but couldn't sleep.

"**G**ood morning! Can I speak to Mr Vayu Iyer?" A female voice asked as Vayu fetched out the mobile from under his pillow.

Vayu had heard that voice before, but his sleepy head couldn't recollect any name or face at that moment. He rubbed his eyes and glanced at the mobile's screen to find an unsaved number of the caller.

"Yes, speaking," he murmured, yawning.

"Sorry to disturb you. This is Poonam, Poonam Nischol. Hope you remember me."

Vayu cleared his throat, made his voice a little heavier to bring more masculinity, and replied, "Of course! I remember you. I have saved your number, but I didn't see the screen...I was asleep so... just picked up... you know."

Vayu was quite surprised by his own behaviour, immature like a teenage lover. He had grown a soft corner for her on their first and only visit. Not only because she was an irresistible stunner, but he liked her fight to grab control of her life and setting up an example of a positive lifestyle. She must be an inspiration for many.

"It's okay. I just called you to convey my gratitude for finding the killer. I hope Di's spirit will rest in peace now. Thank you so much, sir."

"That's our duty, ma'am. And it's yet to be proven in court whether he is guilty or not. We've arrested him based on circumstantial evidence as of now," Vayu explained as he rose from the bed and approached the washroom.

"But you found ricin in those bottles which Dr Khanna had given to Di, isn't it? If that's the case, then what's left to prove?" Poonam was curious.

"Well, there are possibilities that someone else might have tampered with the bottles, either at Shanaya's home or at Dr Khanna's chamber. So, before punishing Dr Khanna, we must consider all these possibilities and do a detailed research," Vayu explained, putting paste on his brush.

"I see. I wish the real culprit gets punished." After a couple of mute seconds, she told with fresh enthusiasm, "By the way, today is my painting exhibition, and I am expecting your precious presence. I hope you can manage a couple of hours from your busy schedule for my paintings."

Vayu took few seconds to suppress the butterflies in his stomach and hid his overenthusiastic unanimity with mature reluctance. "It'll be a pleasure for me. Let's see if I can wrap up my work early today."

"Anyway, do try! I believe my paintings can help you stay away from crime and darkness for at least a few hours," Poonam insisted, laughing softly.

"Sure."

Vayu was thrilled as he started brushing his teeth. Unlike other days, he wore light blue suit and trousers with a white shirt instead of his beloved uniform. He cared to match the colour of his brown shoes with his belt. However, when he looked into the mirror, a shadow of guilt darkened his eyes. He heard his own voice echoing in his mind – justice is not delivered yet. He strongly believed that Dr Khanna was innocent, at least, until he could find a logical motive that could support Abhimanyu's mere conjecture. Hence, he consoled his mind to utilize that whole day in further investigation and only attend the exhibition for a few minutes.

"Did we find anything in Dr Khanna's gadgets that could prove his connection with Shanaya's husband?" Vayu enquired Chaddha as he reached the police station.

Chaddha was busy playing a card game on his mobile. He shook his head, keeping his eyes glued on his mobile screen and replied, "They asked for a week to give us the report."

"When is the first court hearing for Dr Khanna?" Vayu asked impatiently.

"Day after tomorrow," Chaddha answered and shouted looking at the mobile's screen, "*Bhenchod! Sala mujhko harayega.*"

"Shit! So, we have only two days in hand," Vayu murmured and started approaching his desk.

Chaddha took his eyes off from the screen, looked at Vayu, and exclaimed with surprise, "*Arrey* Vayu! What's special today? Is it your birthday?"

Vayu returned to him and replied, "Today evening, I plan to attend Poonam Nischol's painting exhibition. I thought I'd go in civil dress; my uniform might make her other guests a bit uncomfortable, you know. Would you like to join me?"

Vayu made sure to wipe off any tiny hint of a smile from his face while talking about Poonam. And to sound more formal, he added her surname.

"You carry on; I don't understand artsy stuff. Modern art *hai, kuch bhi chalta hai.*" Chaddha made a disgusted face.

Vayu smiled and nodded.

"And just relax for a few days until another big case arrives. Why are you so bothered about the court hearing? It will take months or maybe years to give any verdict. Dr Khanna appointed a famous and successful lawyer. He will definitely come out clean if he is innocent."

Chaddha's words were heavily loaded with his several years of experience. Vayu returned to his desk with a comforted and calmer heart.

Vayu reached Canvas Stories Art Gallery late in the evening. At the entrance, a volunteer gave him a pamphlet. The first fold of that pamphlet had a black and white dual portrait of Shanaya and Poonam and a caption – dedicated to my beloved Di. He felt awkward, thinking of the irony of Poonam's life. That only relationship in her life that she admired, respected, loved, and trusted the most, was a big fat lie. The truth might smash the trust, but that should never make that relation less worthy of admiration, respect or love. According to Vayu, Shanaya was an ideal example of sacrifice, strength, responsibility and altruism which was rare in this modern age.

Vayu mused, "Sometimes, a lie is the best decision that ensures sanity and peace in our future life."

He kept flipping though the glossy pages of that pamphlet, which spoke about the exhibition, the revolutionary art movements of the western world. And there was a short introduction of the artist herself on the last page.

After walking a few more steps, Vayu stepped into a large oval-shaped hall. It had a wooden floor and spotless milky white walls. Enumerable paintings of different sizes and shapes were arranged on the wall. All the large paintings were perfectly placed under the beam of light from a couple of small mounted LED lamps from the ceiling. They were precisely angled to brighten the paintings without any glare. Poonam's guests had been enjoying the inconsequent polite conversation. That was a different India; canapés, wine, expensive watches, jewellery, suits, dresses and sarees.

For a fraction of a second, Vayu was surprised as none of them paid any attention to him. Then he smiled realising he was not in his uniform.

He walked down the hall glancing over the paintings one by one and stopped in front of a painting. He had seen similar paintings in Dr Khanna's office, a mess of overlapping geometrical shapes that kept changing colour on those overlapping portions. Instead of dolphins and eagles in that painting, it had eyes, lips, ears and noses, scattered all over the canvas. The same set of colours had been used to paint both the paintings. The composition of the painting was mysterious. His eyes moved from place to place, unable to decide what the focus of that painting was. He could only imagine that the art reflected the chaos inside the artist. The colours were vivid, almost to the point of garish. It was like a series of paintings condensed onto a single canvas.

"What a pleasant surprise!"

Vayu was startled by that female voice and turned to find Poonam. She was looking stunning in her navy-blue long sequin formal dress. A couple of thin straps ran over her smooth shoulders, holding the low dipped bodice in place, crossed each other on her bare back, and joined the gown at the back of her waist. She had loosely tied her curly hair into a ponytail, letting a few wavy wisps of hair fall over her face. She didn't wear any jewellery or makeup except the lip-gloss. She was irresistible.

Vayu couldn't take his eyes off her until she asked, "You seem interested in this painting."

Vayu nodded, smiling nervously and said, "I have seen a similar painting before, but couldn't understand."

"This is my favourite genre of painting, Cubism. After the invention of the camera, there was no demand for an artist to paint traditional sceneries, family portraits, or objects realistically. Then, Pablo Picasso and Georges Braque invented this genre of art. In this form, an artist explore different ways of looking at the subject of the painting; sometimes from various angles at the same time," she explained, took a glance of Vayu's mused face and continued, "This style is characterized by fragmented subject matter deconstructed in such a way that it can be viewed from multiple angles simultaneously."

"I see," Vayu murmured, observing the painting from different angles. After a few attempts, he shook his head and said, "No, I am not getting anything other than a human face."

"Yes, it is, but fragmented based on different angles," Poonam said with a smile on her face.

She watched Vayu's effort in comprehending that painting for a few seconds. And when she found that the speculation on his face was not lingering, she grabbed his arm and pulled him towards the left side of the painting.

"Look at those pair of eyes, that nose and this truncated pair of lips; just forget about all other figures, lines and colours on this canvas," Poonam instructed, standing close to Vayu.

He could feel the warmth of her body on his forearms. He sniffed the fragrance of her perfume as he nodded and said, "A boy with a wound on his lips. I could see only the blood on his chin, but the wound is not visible from this angle."

Vayu shifted his position to the right of the painting and said, "Yes, there is the wound."

Poonam's face lit up as she told, "Bravo!" Vayu smiled.

"Okay, enjoy yourself. I will be right back after attending to a few more guests."

Vayu moved to the next genre of paintings, called surrealism. Vayu didn't find the genre so difficult to understand, like cubism. Those paintings defied logic and represented a dreamy world of the subconscious mind, but the figures and objects were realistic. As far as Vayu comprehended those paintings, they all represented a deprivation of love and care, and each painting had one character that was responsible for that. Like that mermaid in a painting is the reason for the misery of other realistic fishes in the water.

"If these are the visual representations of Poonam's soul then, she must be a sad soul," Vayu mused, sighing. Vayu looked at Poonam from afar. She was busy explaining a painting to an old man. She caught Vayu's glued eyes on her and smiled; gorgeous. "A gorgeous, unhappy soul."

Vayu walked past those paintings and reached the next genre of paintings on the wall, called realism. As the name suggested, this genre seemed like a photographer had gone out carrying a canvas, brushes, and colours instead of a camera and painted the contemporary normal daily lives to match the same perfection and realism as a photograph.

One of the paintings on a narrow and vertical rectangular canvas attracted Vayu like a magnet. It glued his feet on the floor as he took a close look at it. It seemed like a separated portion of a large painting. It had a half wall-clock at the left edge of the canvas and a back view of a woman with curly hair in front of a door which was ajar. No colour other than black and white had been used in that painting. Vayu kept staring at that paint for a few minutes.

That painting darted a few questions in his mind that made him uncomfortably impatient to look for answers. He pulled out his mobile, and stealthily took a picture of that painting. After bidding a formal goodbye to Poonam for that evening, he rushed towards the exit.

"*Abey* Dubey, I am leaving for the day," Chaddha said loudly, waving as he walked past Dubey's desk.

"Arey, *aap ka to* honeymoon *chal hara hai,* enjoy," Dubey taunted back.

Chaddha returned to his desk and asked, "What are you so busy with?"

Dubey chuckled and said, "I am completely stuck in this Drive Inn murder case. There is no lead, nothing. That witness was the only hope, but you saw that day, how he messed up everything at the last moment." After a thoughtful pause, he complained, "And I don't know why Vayu sir is still busy with that Shanaya murder case. I am not getting any help from him like last time."

"Vayu thinks Dr Khanna is not the killer. I tried my best to convince him that he shouldn't take any case so personally. But young blood… Slowly, he will understand as experience will teach him," Chaddha murmured sighing, and in the next split second, he almost shouted with a toothy grin, "Anyway, I am leaving. Today, Mrs Chaddha has promised to prepare *makki di roti*, *shalgam ki sabzi*, and butter chicken in exchange for a night show after dinner."

They laughed as Chaddha approached the exit. He reached the parking humming a tune with a pleasant smile on his face as he planned to buy some liquor on his way back home. As he rode his bike and started the engine, his mobile vibrated. He fetched out his mobile and saw Vayu's name on the screen. The smile on his face evaporated as he reluctantly received the call.

"Yes, Vayu."

"Chaddha *ji*, come to Dr Khanna's office. I believe I have found something interesting." The excitement in his voice was clear.

"Coming," Chaddha said dully.

The policeman who was in charge to guard Dr Khanna's office was sleeping on his chair when Vayu reached there. He was startled when Vayu patted on his shoulder. He rose from his chair in a hurry and saluted Vayu, stomping his feet.

"Open the door," Vayu ordered.

"I am sorry, sir! *Khali baithe ankh lag gai thi*," he apologised as he took out the key from his trousers' pocket and opened the lock.

Vayu patted on his shoulder and entered the office.

"Switch on the lights!" Vayu order after entering Dr Khanna's large and dark office and walked down to that wall where the painting was fastened.

After few wrong fumbles on the switchboard, that policeman blindly pressed all the switches. Lights flooded the room. Vayu was ready, holding the mobile in his hand. He took a few steps back, looking at the painting on his mobile screen and chuckled. And then, he stood up on the sofa to match the height and clicked a picture. That policeman stood near that switchboard, staring like a curious cat. Vayu hopped down from the sofa and lounged on it, gluing his eyes to the mobile screen. Using a photo editor application, he combined the picture he had taken in Poonam's exhibition with the image of that painting in Dr Khanna's office. He made those half wall-clocks as his point of reference to join them, and in that combined picture, that wall-clock turned into a complete circle. It was evident to Vayu that those two halves were the integral parts of the same wall-clock. A smile waved on Vayu's lips.

In the meanwhile, Chaddha stepped into the room. Vayu indicated the space beside him with a wave of his hand. Chaddha walked down to him and sat on the sofa.

"What do you understand?" Vayu asked, holding the mobile in front of Chaddha's face.

"Vayu, I told you before that I don't understand art at all," Chaddha replied, making a let-me-go expression.

"At least try once, I will help you," Vayu insisted.

Chaddha took a few seconds to study that image and said, "I understand this black and white portion at the right. A girl is peeping through a partly opened door. But this colourful portion at the left is impossible for me to understand." He became silent for a few seconds and said, "It looks like a war between some dolphins and eagles."

"Well done, Chaddha *ji*!" Vayu appreciated laughing and explained, "Suppose you have drawn my face on three separate pieces of tracing papers; one from the front and other two from either side of my face and keep all three paintings together, overlapping. This left portion is like that."

Chaddha nodded thoughtfully and said, "So, to understand one view, we have to remove other views."

"Exactly!" Vayu selected a brush from the tools of that photo editing application and started hiding those eagles and dolphins, painting the background colour on them as he said, "Now we will keep only one dolphin and one eagle and remove the rest."

"But why are we doing this?" Chaddha asked, leaning over the mobile screen.

"This is the master key to open all the closed doors of our investigation," Vayu inattentively murmured, keeping his eyes and fingers busy on the mobile screen.

"What do you see now?" Vayu asked as he finished the editing.

"A necked couple; the woman is sitting on the table, wrapping her legs around the waist and arms around the neck of a man and the man is standing on the floor, grabbing the lower back the woman," Chaddha said a single breath, gazing at the screen.

"Excellent!"

"That eagle and dolphin, are they some kind tattoos on them?" Chaddha asked, taking the mobile from Vayu's hand.

"That dolphin is a pendant. And that eagle must be a tattoo, but we will have to confirm."

"Who are they?"

Vayu answered, pointing his finger on the screen, "The naked woman in the picture is Shanaya. I have seen her wearing that pendant. That man is Dr Khanna, and that woman with curly hair is the artist of this painting, Poonam."

"Okay, you are relating Shanaya by that dolphin pendant, but what about Dr Khanna and Poonam?"

Vayu took his mobile back from Chaddha, slipped it into his pocket, and said, "Everything is connected. I got the image of this black and white painting from Poonam's exhibition. Now, turn back and see that large antique wall clock behind you."

Chaddha turned back and exclaimed, "Oh, this is the painting of this room!"

Vayu nodded and murmured, "One thing you can't hide... is when you're crippled inside."

"Hanji?"

"Nothing, a quote by John Lennon. Let's go! We must meet Dr Khanna about that eagle and his acquaintance with Poonam. Both never mentioned that they even know each other."

"But what does that prove?" Chaddha asked as he got up from the sofa and followed Vayu towards the exit.

"Nothing yet. But this painting talks about the strong motives of both Poonam and Dr Khanna."

The landline on Chaddha's desk had rung for a few minutes before becoming silent. Dubey looked at it from the corner of his eyes, chuckled in irritation, and concentrated back on his work. After a few seconds, it started ringing again. Dubey got up from his chair, throwing the pen on the table in irritation, reached Chaddha's desk, and picked up the receiver.

"Hello, Sub-inspector Dubey from Noida police station."

"Hello, Dubey *ji*, Inspector Junaid Alam from Bhopani police station, Faridabad. Good evening."

"Good evening, Inspector Junaid. How can I help you?" Dubey asked, pulling Chaddha's chair to give some rest to his tired legs.

"A man named Suraj Kumar turned in today; resident of Jasana. According to his statement, he had been offered money to murder the daughter of DGP Kolkata, Ahi Chatterjee."

A shiver ran down Dubey's spine, twisting his tongue.

"I had read about that case in newspapers. So I thought it will be better to inform you before starting any investigation."

"Ye...yes. That's a good decision. I will visit your police station tomorrow morning."

Dubey kept the receiver plunging himself into deep thought.

"You go ahead! I will join you after finishing this formality," Chaddha suggested at the jail entrance and started filling up all the details in the register.

Vayu started walking through a long and narrow corridor, nodding his head to every salute by the passing policemen and stopped in front of Dr Khanna's cell. Dr Khanna was reading a book in a white long kurta and pyjama; he hadn't been given the prisoner's uniform till then. Even in that dark, small and filthy concrete box, he sat like a king on the floor.

"Dr Khanna, can we talk?" Vayu asked politely.

Dr Khanna glanced at Vayu, flipped a page and started reading it. After a few seconds, he said, "Talk to my lawyer; I have nothing for you."

"Dr Khanna, if you are not guilty of murder, this conversation will help you the most in this world. So, please cooperate. And if you don't, my belief will be further stronger against you. The choice is yours."

Vayu played his psychology card, and that worked. "What do you want to know? You already have those recordings of my sessions, and that has Shanaya's whole life," Dr Khanna snapped back, tossing the book aside.

"How do you know Poonam? Poonam Nischol?"

"Shanaya had brought her to me for counselling. That time, I had only formal acquaintance with Shanaya; just a guardian of my patient," Dr Khanna replied reluctantly and countered, "But how is that connected to Shanaya's murder?"

"How was your relationship with Poonam? I mean, was that just a formal one, how it is supposed to be between a patient and a psychologist? Or did it gradually turn into a romantic one?" Vayu enquired, gluing his eyes on Dr Khanna's face.

Dr Khanna laughed, not spontaneously but to mock Vayu. And then his face contorted in anger as he said, "Don't judge the whole world through the lens of your own mentality. I am a professional and involving myself in any kind of relationship with my patients is unethical, according to my principles."

In the meanwhile, Chaddha had reached there.

Vayu smirked and asked, "What happened to your principle when you had sex with Shanaya in your office?"

"Wh...what rubbish!" Dr Khanna fumbled.

Vayu held the edited painting in front of his eyes and asked, "There was someone who had been watching you two, and that vision wounded her heart so deeply that she could paint this and gift it to you. Can you identify your tattoo?"

"Poonam!" Dr Khanna whispered. "But I never showed any inclination or interest toward her. I had no such intention for Shanaya either; it just happened only once... that too in spontaneity. You know, we just got carried away in the moment."

"Yeah, it might be one-sided."

Dr Khanna kept standing there in silence, holding the iron bars of the cell, and after a few moments, he pleaded, "Believe me, I didn't kill Shanaya!"

"Let's see." Vayu's voice was loaded with confidence, and a glow of accomplishment lit up his face as he started walking towards to exit. However, after a few steps, he returned to Dr Khanna's cell tagging along with Chaddha and asked, "Does Poonam have split personality disorder?"

"Yes. Poonam needed serious medication. So, I had referred her to a psychiatrist. But how do you know that?"

"That Buddha's painting in your reception area; I guess, that's her painting too," Vayu replied with a smile.

Dr Khanna nodded a yes.

Vayu started walking towards the exit; Chaddha followed.

Chaddha somehow managed to suppress the butterflies in his stomach until they reached the street outside the jail and asked, "So, have we reached the closure of this investigation?"

"I guess so. But we don't even have any circumstantial evidence," Vayu replied, thoughtfully twisting his moustache.

Chaddha kept on staring at Vayu with a helpless expression and waited for his next words.

"We just need a confession; I don't see any other way around," Vayu whispered. The wrinkles on his forehead were stating the uncertainty of the success.

"But what would make the killer confess?" Chaddha asked impatiently.

Vayu became silent for seconds and told, "Guilt. I have a weapon to inject guilt in the killer's mind, and I hope it works."

The next morning, Chaddha had been waiting for Vayu outside the police station.

"All of them have arrived," Chaddha informed as soon as Vayu reached near the entrance.

"Good job!" Vayu appreciated, smiling.

Chaddha responded to the appreciation with a proud smile. They reached Vayu's desk in a hurry where Manoj Sharma, Poonam Nischol, Rizwan Ahmed, Supriya Sinha and Jignesh Patel had been eagerly waiting for Vayu. Chaddha had to pull a few chairs from a few of his colleagues' desks to make that sitting arrangement for them. Vayu glanced at their eyes as he took his seat; all of them were overwhelmed with questions.

"Good morning, everyone! So, you all might have heard that Dr Khanna has been charged with the murder of Mrs Shanaya Mehta. Though it's yet to be proven in court, but we are confident of our investigation," Vayu told, minutely reading their faces, and as he expected, everyone seemed relaxed after hearing Vayu.

"Then, why are we wasting time here?" Jignesh asked in annoyance.

"I just wanted to convey my perception about Shanaya to all of you, just as a human being. Yes, I know, this is not my duty. From this entire investigation, I have learnt that all of you have some negative opinions about her, except Poonam and Jignesh," Vayu replied.

After exchanging a glance with Poonam, Vayu continued, "According to Supriya, she was a bitch. Sandy called her a whore. She was a cheater to her husband Manoj, and betrayer to Rizwan. Though I haven't heard Jignesh addressing her with any such words, she was just the trophy he had lost in his college days. It was only Poonam who actually admired, respected, loved and trusted her."

Vayu became silent as he rose from his chair, observing Poonam. Her eyes were covered with a film of tears.

Manoj mocked, laughing, "After so many years of spending my life under the same roof with her, I have to learn from you how she was? Funny!"

"Yes, it is funny that even after so many years, you couldn't make that comfort zone for her to share her problems with you. Because you were always in some trouble or the other, and never emerged as her support," Vayu retorted as he walked close to Manoj.

Manoj became silent.

"What's your perception about her?" Rizwan asked.

"She was an ideal example of sacrifice, strength, responsibility and altruism. And I believe none of you except Poonam comprehend that. Yesterday, I went to Poonam's painting exhibition and learnt that she has dedicated her exhibition to her elder sister, Shanaya."

Tears overflowed from Poonam's eyes as she rose from the chair and asked, "May I leave now?"

"I know it's difficult for you to acknowledge that she is no more. But please have your seat. I am almost done," Vayu requested softly as he stood close to her.

Poonam sat back reluctantly.

Supriya was listening to all that silently till then. But she couldn't keep quiet anymore and asked, "What made you have that great perception of Shanaya?"

Vayu smiled as he returned to his chair and said, "She swallowed poison just so you could live a guilt-free life, especially for Rizwan, Manoj and Poonam."

"What?" Poonam asked, wiping the tears from her face.

"Your father, Pranav Nischol blackmailed Shanaya and raped her. He threatened her that if she didn't agree, he won't pay the expenses for her mother's treatment. And…"

Poonam cut him short and screamed, "You are lying!"

Her voice was loud enough to draw the attention of all the people present in the police station.

Vayu pulled out his mobile from his trousers' pocket, played that particular portion of Shanaya's counselling where she had spoken about her rape, and held the mobile up in the air for everyone's viewing.

'Guilt is a feeling of responsibility for having done something wrong. In its healthiest form, guilt is a moral compass that guides us to not repeat the same behaviour that we consider wrong. But, the guilt closely related to shame doesn't feel good: mentally replaying what happened, wishing you could go back and change what happened,' Vayu mused, gazing at Poonam.

As the video progressed, the guilt on Poonam's face became more vivid. Her conscience was affected slowly with the toxicity, needing no more than a spark to set it ablaze. The fire burnt her out so badly there was nothing left but a shell, an outline of a person. The tip of her nose, cheeks, and earlobes turned red as she felt an incessant throb in her heart, pleading her to confess. She felt a blend of sorrow, anxiety, shame and an intense desire to make amends. But it was too late for that.

She burst into tears and screamed, "She is a liar. She is just trying to demean my father."

"And what could be her motive, according to you? After several years of your father's death, what is she trying to achieve, lying in a confidential conversation with a therapist?" Vayu questioned as he walked up to Poonam and gave her a piece of paper.

"This is your original birth certificate, an unaltered one," Vayu told.

Vayu stopped the video, kept the mobile back into his pocket. She was weeping inconsolably then.

Vayu whispered close to her ear, "Speak up, let it come out! You will feel better."

"She was the apple of everyone's eyes. People never used to get tired of appreciating her beauty, intelligence, kindness and success in business... In any family gathering or social functions, she was the show-stealer, the centre of attention. She was everywhere in my small world – TV, magazines, radio... Sometimes, I doubted my existence in anyone's lives around me, as if I was some invisible spirit. I started doubting my self-worth, and gradually that feeling of inferiority became the fixed state of my mind. And the worst thing was, I had no one other than her who could help me come out of that mental mess. Again, she had proved her superiority. I started hating my life and attempted suicide a few times."

She kept on fumbling, weeping and shivering as she continued, "Th...Then I met Dr Khanna, the first person in my life who heard me with his complete attention. I started liking every moment spent with him. Falling in love with him was like entering a house and finally realizing I'm home. When he smiled at me, I felt his invisible hands wrapping around me, making me feel safe. When his eyes were locked into m...mine, I could see galaxies instead of just pupils. Having him in my life made me feel like everything was possible in this world; I could conquer anything."

She became silent for a moment and murmured, "She snatched him too from me and compelled me to plan all this against both of them." She looked up, eyes bloodshot, "Yes, I killed Shanaya."

Everyone looked at her in awestricken silence.

Vayu gestured at Chaddha to arrest her. He wiped the drop of tear at the corner of his eyes as he left the room.

Epilogue

It was snowing heavily in Chicago. From that large window that occupied the entire wall at the fortieth floor of the 1407 On Michigan Avenue, nothing was visible other than the swirling flakes. The snow became so thick that the trees appeared as confetti... as if they were the flakes that danced.

She hummed Tagore's song – *Tumi robe nirobe hridoye momo*, sitting by that large window. That blizzard outside was so strong that her familiar and favourite sight of Michigan lake at the horizon had erased. As she looked upwards, she felt as if she was flying upward rather than watching the crystals fall towards her.

"Ahi, your coffee is ready," her roomie announced from the kitchen.